OVERRIDING THE DARKNESS

Diane Winters

First published in 2025 by Blossom Spring Publishing
Overriding The Darkness © 2025 Diane Winters
ISBN 978-1-0684329-4-1
E: admin@blossomspringpublishing.com
W: www.blossomspringpublishing.com

1

If I walked away from everything, no one would blame me. Over a short period of time, my life took many turns, stops, and even a backward step or two. I dared not look to a future that could hold more of the same. My friends said I'd gone through more than my share of grief, and, surely, my life would improve, given enough time. No one knows how much time they are given, and my life is proof of that. It took three years before I decided to let go of my grief and begin to live again. I just wasn't sure how. That's where my cousin, Jackie, came into the picture. Taking me by the hand, she led me to the safety of her home and lifted me out of my wallowing pit of despair. She saved me, literally. Facing my fears with Jackie beside me, I began to look to the future, instead of stagnating in the past.

2

Like most typical newly married couples, Liza and Jason started their life together full of dreams of their future. They had new jobs and careers to build, and they were loving every moment. Liza was hired by the company that she interned with while still in college, and she knew that advancement would be well-earned. Every day was an adventure, as the couple settled into their routines. Both were doing well at work, and Liza's corporate boss began to notice. But not for the work she was doing. He stopped by group meetings and watched the dynamics of the staff, then he would silently leave. One day, he stopped by Liza's desk.

"Ms. Augustine, I hear good things about your work, and I'm impressed when I watch you interact with others on your team. Keep this up, and you'll be getting a promotion in no time."

"Thank you, sir. I appreciate the feedback."

Mr. Davenport smiled and checked out all of Liza's features before leaving her cubicle. She felt uncomfortable but shrugged it off to her nervousness. After all, she should feel honored that the boss recognized her hard work. She heard murmurings in the room but shut them out and went back to work. Mr. Davenport would stop by Liza's desk once a month or so, always complimenting her on a job well done. Employed for a couple of years now, she was often made a lead on many projects. Her immediate supervisors all knew that Liza would go far, and her evaluations proved her worth to the company. The bonuses weren't bad, either. During her third year of employment, one of her supervisors decided to retire and recommended Liza to be promoted to his position. It was no surprise to her when she got a call from Mr. Davenport's secretary to come to his office.

"Thank you for coming, Ms. Augustine."

"Thank you, sir." She sat down in the cushy chair opposite the desk and wiped her sweaty palms on her skirt.

"So, Ms. Augustine, David says you would be a great replacement when he retires. I've been noticing you for quite some time now, and he's probably correct. But I need to discuss the job more thoroughly with you if you genuinely want this promotion."

"Yes sir. I'm very interested in finding out more about the job. Would David be willing to train me?"

"I'm sure he would be delighted. But first, I need you to understand there are some stipulations to getting the job."

"Oh? Like what?"

He leered at her and smirked. "How about we discuss this tonight over supper? Say, seven at the Cottonwood Hotel, suite 204. If you don't arrive, I will assume you aren't interested in the job."

Liza blinked several times before standing up. "I understand sir. I better get back to work."

She practically ran from the room and back to her office space, not believing what she heard. It was almost time to leave for the day, so she clocked out and went home early. She was still sitting in a fog when Jason walked in the door. He listened as she told him what happened. He was so mad he threatened to go and beat the man to a pulp.

After much discussion, they agreed she would go to

work and forget about the promotion. After all, they were trying to start a family. Jason ordered delivery for their evening meal, and after discussing the pros and cons, they both felt they made the right decision. Besides, if she said anything now, it would be the boss's word against hers. Next time, she would be better prepared. The following day, Liza arrived for work and spent the better part of her time in meetings. At three, she received word that Mr. Davenport wanted to see her again. This time, she went to the office knowing what to expect. Her phone was in her jacket breast pocket, the camera was pointed toward Mr. Davenport upon her arrival.

"Ms. Augustine, I'm so sorry you missed out on a lovely supper last evening. And I'm very disappointed in you for doing so."

"Yes, sir. I'm sure you were. But it was my understanding that if I didn't show up it was because I didn't want the promotion. I discussed it with my husband, and we decided I wasn't in any hurry for advancement at this time."

"I see. Well, that's where you misunderstood me, my dear. What I meant was that you either show up to my suite, or you don't have a job. Period."

"Mr. Davenport, you never mentioned to me that I would be fired for not coming to your suite."

He laughed. "Listen, sweetheart. When I invite you to my suite, I expect full compliance. Now. You have two days to decide which one it is. Your job or unemployment. I will be in my suite on Friday evening. Be there or pack up your desk. And if you don't show up, you will never be able to get another job like this around town. I'll see to it."

"I understand, Mr. Davenport. Good day."

4

Chuckling, he replied, "See you Friday, my dear."

On shaking legs, Liza left his office and went into the first ladies' room she came to. Stopping the filming, she took some deep breaths. Lately, she'd been hearing more and more gossip about Mr. Davenport. Now she knew it was all true. Returning to her desk, she began emptying personal belongings into her purse. Grateful she'd brought an oversized bag that day, Liza didn't want to appear too obvious. She planned to finish her week, tidy up some work, and then see what Monday brought. At least Jason was supportive on the matter.

On Friday, anything else that was personal was packed away. Double checking, she shut off the computer and walked out the door. Jason was going to take her away for the weekend and had also made an appointment with their lawyer to begin a lawsuit. The appointment wasn't for another couple of weeks, and she was told not to show the video to anyone until the lawyer reviewed the evidence. The couple spent the weekend relaxing by the seashore, taking long walks, and talking about their hopes for the future. Liza knew she would get another job even though Mr. Davenport threatened her. Their lawyer reassured her of that.

Monday morning, Liza barely entered the building before being escorted to the human resource department. There, she was fired for insubordination. She almost laughed in their face but asked for the paperwork to file a sexual harassment charge. After filling out and signing all the paperwork, she asked for copies before turning in her badge and key. They explained she would be escorted to her desk to pick up her personal items, but Liza smiled and said it wouldn't be necessary and that she would be leaving the building immediately. Liza called and left

Jason a message, then went to see her parents for the day. She was home and had supper about ready when Jason arrived. She smiled and gave him a big kiss.

"Welcome home to your unemployed wife."

"You don't look too devastated."

"Actually, I'm not, right now. I'm mad at the situation. Once I talked to my parents, they agreed we are taking the right path. We need to expose him to the public because the HR department might sweep it under the rug."

"Payback."

"Yip. Let's eat."

Time flew by, and Liza was finally sitting across from the lawyer. She told Jason that she could handle the situation and he could go on to work. The video was watched twice, then they went over the copy of the paperwork she received from the HR department on the day she was fired for insubordination. Liza also made sure a copy of her sexual harassment complaint was included. As the lawyer began laying out the lawsuit that he would eventually file, her phone buzzed. Glancing down, she was startled to see a number from the police department.

"Excuse me a second." She hit the accept button. "Hello?"

"Ms. Augustine, this is Officer Ryan. We need you to go to the hospital immediately. Your husband was in a multi-car pileup on the interstate. I don't know his condition."

"Yes, sir. Oh my god." She looked at the lawyer. "I've got to go. Jason's been in a terrible accident."

Flying out the door, she wasn't sure how she managed to get to the hospital without getting in a wreck, herself. She was escorted to his bedside and couldn't believe her eyes.

"Jason. Oh, Jason."

Barely conscious, he managed to say he loved her, and they kissed. A few minutes later, he was gone. The doctors worked on him but told her there was too much damage. In a state of shock, she sat in the waiting room, where there were several other distraught family members. Liza finally called Jason's parents. She asked that Jason not be moved until they got there, and the staff was more than happy to comply, as they had their hands full. Jason's wouldn't be the only death from the accident that day. She eventually called her parents, and they rushed over, too. Once everyone said their goodbyes, Liza went home with her parents. Her father drove her car while she stared out the window. She knew nothing would ever be the same again.

After the funeral, Liza returned home. There she sat, day after day, staring blankly at the walls or fingering Jason's belongings. Seeing her not coping, her parents worried about her constantly. Two weeks after the funeral, she called her mother to come get her because Liza was in terrible pain. They went to the emergency room where she subsequently miscarried. The couple didn't know she was pregnant. Totally devastated all over again and losing the last remaining piece of Jason, Liza completely fell apart. Her mother moved her back in with them, and eventually, Liza recovered enough to try living on her own again.

Several months later, she was finally becoming used to being by herself and maintaining the apartment. Jason's insurance payout was double indemnity because of the car accident, and it was enough to pay all of the expenses of the funeral, with enough left over to pay for the apartment a year in advance. Between their savings and what was left from insurance, Liza would be okay financially for the next several months, as long as she was careful.

Now she was thinking about finding a job, which made her wonder about her old company and the lawsuit left hanging the day Jason died. She contemplated making another appointment with the lawyer but called an old co-worker, Angie, first, to see if anything had changed. They went out to supper, and Angie explained everything that had gone down. Shortly after her firing, word got out that Liza had filed a sexual harassment charge. Two other women ended up filing a lawsuit against Mr. Davenport and the company. The board of directors fired Mr. Davenport, and when the details came out, his wife filed for a divorce, too. Rumors were that he was living in the suite that he had been luring his victims to.

Angie and other co-workers used to hide from Mr. Davenport if they knew he was coming around. She stated she was sorry that they hadn't warned her, but everyone was excited when David mentioned she was going to be their new supervisor. They were devastated when they heard about her being fired but knew exactly what had happened and were glad that Liza hadn't fallen for the man's devious nature.

Her lawyer took the file, which included the video, and filed a lawsuit on behalf of Liza. He knew that, if there was one, there were more. All he had to do was wait and keep digging. He didn't have to wait long. Within a couple of months, he ended up with a nice extensive list to go after the slimeball, of which two also had evidence. The lawyer dedicated most of his hours to the case when he found out that the HR department had shredded Liza's sexual harassment complaint instead of investigating it. Turns out, they had been victims of Mr. Davenport themselves and didn't want to lose their jobs. The women were placed on probation and someone else was hired to supervise the office. Feeling justice was served, Liza sent a personal thank-you note to her lawyer.

About a year after the accident, Liza received a letter in the mail, discussing a class action lawsuit against the estate of the car's driver, that caused the multi-car pileup. Liza's lawyer was involved in helping her obtain a settlement for the man causing Jason's death. Evidently, his parents touched base with him after the funeral, to see if he could do something. There were enough cam videos from several people's cars to show how the man caused the start of the wreck from road rage. He slammed into another vehicle, which, in turn, rolled. Then the man lost control of his vehicle, too. So many people couldn't stop in time and slammed into the two vehicles. The mess caused a chain reaction. The drivers of the two vehicles died on impact, followed by four other deaths and multiple injuries. It was going to be a slow process, but the lawsuit was definitely valid.

3

Things had settled into a routine for Liza over time, and she was updating her resume. Needing to talk to her parents about Sunday lunch, she called several times and got no answer. Normally, one or the other would answer the phone, and she was sure they wouldn't leave town without telling her. She finally drove over to the house and noticed the cars in the drive. Letting herself into the house, Liza called out their names several times as she went from room to room. She found them in bed, gone. Becoming dizzy, Liza rushed out of the house before she fainted. She blamed it on the sight of her parents. Even their little dog was gone, lying there at the foot of the bed.

Liza called the police immediately while she sat on the curbside, taking some deep breaths. The officers realized something was wrong in the house and called the fire department. The house was full of carbon monoxide, and at such a level no one could survive. Everyone reassured Liza that they fell asleep and never woke up, not realizing what was happening.

After the funeral, she and her brother, who was in the service, hired someone to repair everything wrong with the house, so they could sell it. Several items needed to be looked after, and it would take some time to complete all the projects. Liza was still living in her apartment, and since she wasn't working yet, it fell to her to manage the repairs.

Six months later, her brother was killed overseas by an IED. That was the last straw. Liza's brain shut down, and her cousin Jackie took her to the hospital. She spent three days staring at the walls. Once the doctor began talking about committing her to a mental health unit, she became upset and requested to go home. There were too many things to do, and being locked up wasn't going to help get it done. Against his better judgment, the doctor discharged Liza on a high dose of medications and demanded she follow up for outpatient care.

Cousin Jackie stayed in constant contact with Liza over the last couple of years and made sure she was there for her after each catastrophe. They had been thick as thieves growing up. Even though they had gone their separate ways when they were older, they stayed in touch like sisters. They even stood up for each other at their weddings. Liza always knew she could count on Jackie to be there for her. Too bad she wasn't up to reciprocating these days.

Crying all night, Liza cleaned out her parents' house by day. There was nothing like the fear of being committed to make a person act normal around others. She wasn't normal. Far from it. She eventually gave up the apartment and moved back into her childhood home. Going through Jason's belongings, and then her parents', was much easier that way. She no longer had a job, a husband, or a family. Her parents left a little nest egg, and she used some of that for the much-needed repairs. The army sent her brother's belongings back to the house, but there wasn't much in that cardboard box. His life insurance money was put in her savings account. When he returned home on leave, he would always stay at the house with their parents. She left the box in his room to go through later.

Liza could only deal with one death at a time. Jason's

belongings were first. There were a few things she thought his parents might like, and they were pleased to pick them up. They spent a little time crying on each other's shoulders again, but it didn't seem to help Liza at all. She was so tired of spending tears and wondered how there were any left.

After the major repairs were completed on the house, she began to paint all the walls and sell off the furniture. Everything took time, and Liza was in no hurry. Between Jason's insurance policy, the small settlement she received from her old company, the lawsuit from the accident, and the dab of money left from her parents' savings, Liza managed to live day-to-day. As the days ticked by and after the payment of all the repair bills, Liza's money was slowly disappearing. But the tears had finally stopped.

Running out of things to do to the house, Liza listed it with the realtor. The house sold within a couple of months. Now she didn't have any place to go. She stood in the yard, looking at her childhood home, seeing the "sold" sign, and knew she needed to make some life-altering changes immediately. She wasted a lot of years, and it was time to step up. Now that Liza decided to start her life over, Jackie was right there. She and Ray invited her to stay with them until she figured out where to live and work.

Packing a suitcase, Liza took a few boxes of mementos to her car. After one final look at the house, she locked the door with the keys inside. She hoped the new owners would appreciate her hard work updating the home. She hopped into her car and headed over to Jackie's. Liza was grateful for the love and care her cousin provided to her, and was glad she and Ray were so welcoming to invite her into their home for the time being. They had plenty of room since Jackie had been unable to have children yet. Pulling up in front of the house, she unloaded her boxes into the garage, out of the way. Then she picked up her suitcase and headed up the stairs to her new bedroom. Looking around, she sighed before unpacking. Putting her shampoo and other items in the bathroom, Liza stopped and looked in the mirror. She did a double-take when she didn't recognize the person looking back. Disgusted, she flipped off the light and went back downstairs to wait for Jackie to come home from work.

In the coming days, Liza settled into a new routine. Mostly, she tried not to get in Jackie and Ray's way, and she certainly didn't want to overstay her welcome. Ray went to his friend Cliff's to watch sports, and Jackie and Liza went shopping. A fair trade-off, they thought. She had only been living with them a couple of weeks when Ray's birthday arrived. They planned to go out for supper to celebrate, and Ray invited his friend Cliff. It didn't matter to Liza. Still in a slump and not knowing how to get out of it yet, she went along with whatever Jackie wanted.

4

Sitting in his car, staring blankly through the windshield, Cliff finally shook himself, started the car, and headed out. Chuckling, he wondered if his nosy neighbor was trying to figure out why he got into his car and then didn't go anywhere. His best friends were Ray and Jackie, and they had invited him out for a birthday supper, and Ray casually mentioned that Jackie's cousin was staying with them for a few weeks. Liza would be going with them to supper and hoped he wouldn't mind. What could he say? It was Ray's birthday, so of course he would go. After all, they didn't have to invite him to come along. But Cliff figured the couple would try and set up this Liza girl as his date since they had tried to do so in the past with other women. That's why he sat in the driveway, trying to figure out how to call and say he couldn't make it at the last minute. But the restaurant was one of his favorites, so he guessed he could manage to get through one evening no matter what.

Running late, he pulled up to the house and honked to let his friends know he had arrived. The girls got in the backseat, and Ray in the front. Introductions were made, and Cliff turned the car toward the restaurant. Zipping through traffic, he didn't want to be late for their reservation. After all, it would have been his fault if they were. He and Ray talked about the ballgames that would be televised that weekend and ignored the women in the backseat. He glanced in his rearview mirror a couple of times at the stranger and saw a pale, unbecoming woman. She looked nothing like her vivacious cousin.

Once seated at their table, Liza sat quietly and concentrated on her menu as the three friends conversed. The group had been there many times before and already knew what they wanted. The waitress took their orders, and the conversation continued without Liza's input. Jackie drew her into a conversation of their own, and let the men chat about sports. It wasn't until Liza was halfway through her meal that Cliff addressed her directly.

"How's your salmon?"

Liza's fork stopped mid-air, she blinked a couple of times and then answered. "It's delicious. Thanks for asking."

Cliff nodded and turned back to his steak. Liza shook her head and continued eating. Jackie chuckled and whispered, "Great conversationalist." Even Liza laughed.

Cliff dropped everyone off, waved, and took off like a shot, for home. Ray stood watching the car fly down the street. "What's up with him tonight?"

Jackie took his arm as they followed Liza into the house. "I bet he was afraid we were trying to hook him up with Liza. You probably should have told him we had nothing like that in mind when you invited him to supper."

"Shoot. It didn't even occur to me."

A rare smile crossed Liza's face. "I'll head upstairs. Thanks for taking me with you. Happy birthday, Ray."

"Thanks. And I'm sorry about Cliff's behavior. He's usually a perfect gentleman."

Shrugging her shoulders, she began her trek upstairs and called back over her shoulder. "It was actually kind of funny, now that you mention the reason. Goodnight."

After a nightcap, Ray sat on the couch, holding Jackie

on his lap. "I don't blame Cliff for believing we were setting him up on a blind date since we did it in the past."

"I know, but I didn't realize you hadn't said anything to him, and by the time I figured it out, I decided to enjoy his discomfort. I should have told Liza, though. Maybe she could have helped make him more uncomfortable."

"You're just plain mean, sweetheart." Kissing his wife, he scooted her off his lap and got up, pulling her with him. "Let's get to bed. Maybe I'll call him tomorrow to explain. Or maybe not."

"Now who is being mean?" They both laughed.

Cliff pulled into his driveway, relieved that the night was over. He spent much of the time ignoring Jackie's cousin and hoped they all got the message that he wasn't interested. Especially a mousy girl like that.

From the time that Liza moved into her cousin's home, Jackie insisted on getting Liza on the road to being healthier. The stress and depression made the poor girl unhealthy. Jackie cooked every evening and left fresh fruit and vegetables for Liza during the day, along with sandwich makings. Then in the evenings, after the supper mess was cleaned up, they went for long walks when the weather cooperated. More importantly, an appointment was made with Jackie's doctor to discuss Liza's medication and history of depression.

By the time Liza moved in with Jackie, she had lost thirty pounds, her hair was falling out, and her cheeks were sallow. With her skin so pale, she was not a pretty sight. Jackie started Liza on a regimen of vitamins and exercise, and she was beginning to look and feel better. But the sluggishness never seemed to go away. Hence, a doctor's appointment was made. After a long visit with Liza, he decided to back her off the anti-depressant. He felt that it was much too high and that she would feel better at a lower dose. He promised to work with her over time to find the appropriate dosage, plus strongly encouraged her to continue with a healthy diet and exercise plan that Jackie had developed. He was happy with the vitamin intake and felt that Liza would see an improvement in a few short weeks. Dr. Moline was a pleasant man, and she could see why Jackie trusted his opinion. Liza made another appointment on her way out.

Two months later, Liza was sitting in the kitchen, listening to the creaks and groans of an empty house while Jackie was at work. The back porch was the perfect setting to read the want ads in the local paper. She sat in a rocker and felt sorry for herself instead. Pretending to be strong, inside Liza felt a mess. Her stomach growled which made her come out of her stupor. Fixing a sandwich, she threw her shoulders back and shook herself in disgust. Her moods were certainly all over the place. The newspaper didn't have any jobs she was qualified for, so Liza checked online. Taking a drink to wash down the sandwich, she filled out her resume and posted it to a couple of job sites.

Not more than two hours later, she began to get messages about job availability. Most were spam emails, but she sorted through the mail until she found a couple that were appropriate job requests. When Jackie arrived home from work, they chatted about their day while preparing a meal. Ray rolled in about the time supper was ready. For entertainment, Liza read some of the responses to her resume. Ray and Jackie gave Liza a tough time about her call-girl and sugar daddy requests and thought she should investigate them further.

The following day, Liza spent several hours

investigating the background of the companies that had shown an interest in her resume. After responding to a couple and setting up appointments for interviews, she went to her room to decide on the right outfit. Nothing fit. With the loss of weight, everything was much too large for her. Now that she was eating decent meals, she had gained back fifteen pounds of the thirty she had lost and thought she was at a good weight to maintain. She tried to look at needing new clothes as a good thing.

Listening to Liza complain about needing new work outfits and what it was going to cost her, Jackie had just the answer for her. There was a second-hand shop in the mall that catered to working women. They drove over on that Saturday, and Liza tried on several outfits. Pleased with what size she was going to be able to wear, she went overboard a little bit. Then they went to a few other shops for shoes, jeans, shirts, and sweaters. Liza's bank account took a big hit that day, but she hadn't spent money on herself for years.

Once home, the women went through Liza's closet and drawers and threw away old baggy clothes that had seen better days. Then they packed up the oversized business wear to donate back to the second-hand shop. All of her new items were washed, dried, and put away. It had been a long time since Liza felt good about herself. Dressing in well-fitting clothes, even casuals, made her feel a lot better about herself. In a couple of days, she had an appointment to have her hair done. The vitamins had done the trick, and her hair was no longer falling out. Looking in the mirror, Liza thought she finally recognized the woman looking back. Smiling, she shut off the light and went downstairs to help with supper.

With her hair cut and styled, wearing a new business

suit, Liza felt good as she walked in for her interviews. She needed to explain the gaps in her work history but was able to hold her own in the interviews and knew she nailed them. She did have a preference over which company she wanted to work for. All she could do was cross her fingers while she waited. She didn't have to wait long. By the next week, she was offered a great position at a company across town from Jackie's home. Once she went in and filled out the paperwork, her next step was finding an apartment.

Jackie and Liza spent a Saturday looking at a few openings. There were some that, when they drove up, they kept on driving. Finally, as they were shown an apartment fairly close to her work, Liza was impressed. Only a few years old, the place looked and felt like home. Looking out the back patio doors, she saw a park close by with hiking trails. When the weather was bad, she could use the gym on the lower floor. The best thing about it was the washer and dryer in the apartment itself. She wouldn't have to use a communal space. It was perfect for her, and she took it on the spot.

They went furniture shopping and arranged for a delivery time. Outside of those few boxes of keepsakes, Liza walked away from her past without any belongings. Starting anew was simply fine with her, as she felt that, in reality, she was starting from scratch. Jackie helped organize the apartment and made sure she had food and cleaning supplies. They were both teary-eyed when Liza closed the door behind Jackie. But being only twenty minutes away was a blessing and they knew they would still spend a lot of time together.

Liza had been so busy the last few weeks that she didn't even have time to be sad or melancholic. Stepping away from the closed door, she walked around the apartment, touching and adjusting items. Her savings had taken quite a hit once Liza paid the rent and bought furnishings, along with her new wardrobe. She felt that she was finally adjusting to her new life. Maybe she was recovering after all. It was way past time.

5

A few months later, Jackie called and talked with so much excitement that Liza could barely understand anything she said.

"Wait. What? You guys are going to have a baby?"

"Yes. Isn't it exciting?"

"That's wonderful. I know you two had all but given up."

"Oh, Liza, I'm so scared. After all these years, I don't want anything to go wrong."

"It will be fine. We need to celebrate in style."

"We plan to throw a big party here, at the house, but only after I'm far enough along that I'm sure the baby is okay."

They talked for several more minutes and Liza promised to help with the party whenever Jackie and Ray decided it was appropriate. They met up on the weekend and made several lists, which was one of Jackie's favorite things to do. When Jackie finally settled on a date for the BBQ, it was only because Dr. Moline had repeatedly told her the baby was developing fine, and everyone was healthy. At work, Liza mentioned the BBQ to her team, and Pierre asked what the party entailed. He was intrigued by the explanation.

"That sounds like a fun time. Would you care if I went, too? I'd like to experience a BBQ." Pierre was only in town for a few months while the company worked on a special project and would be going home to France soon.

"Jackie won't care. You can be my plus one."

"Plus one?"

"My date."

"Very good. I would like that."

"I'll write down the address for you because I'll be over there early in the afternoon to help set up. When you arrive, text me and I'll meet you at the door."

"I'm so excited." The whole group laughed at Pierre's obvious thrill at being invited to the BBQ. Well, technically he invited himself.

Jackie and Ray's place was busy from noon on. Preparation of food kept the kitchen busy, grills were set up, tables and chairs were placed, and coolers were full of ice, waiting for drinks. The neighbors were helping, and Liza couldn't believe it when Jackie said they would probably have fifty people show up. Cars were parked around the block and up and down the street, in any opening found. Pierre wondered if he would ever find a place to leave his car but eventually arrived at the right house. Liza hung out in the front yard until he showed up, which helped. Amazed by the turnout, Pierre was quite impressed. Jackie's parents arrived and shooed her out into the backyard with Ray. Once Pierre arrived, Liza wasn't allowed back into the kitchen, either. Pierre stuck to Liza like glue for the first hour or so. They ate, laughed, and ate some more. Ray got an impromptu band together and there was even a little dancing. Somewhere in the middle of all these people was Cliff. He helped Ray at the grill, but eventually, he stopped by to say hello to Liza.

"Liza, it's good to see you. You're looking very pretty this evening."

"Thanks, Cliff." She expected him to wander off, but he nodded toward Pierre.

"Who's your friend?"

Linking arms with Pierre's, Liza replied with a smile. "This is Pierre. Pierre, Cliff. Cliff is best friends with Ray."

"Nice to meet you. Ray has been very hospitable."

Cliff cocked one eyebrow when he heard Pierre's accent. Liza tugged Pierre's arm. "See you later." She offered a little wave and pulled Pierre over to the drink table.

"You don't like Mr. Cliff?"

"Let's just say he hasn't been very friendly toward me before, so I didn't feel like giving him the time of day now." Then she added, "It's not important. Want to dance?"

"Sure thing." They set their drinks down and wandered over to an open spot to dance.

Cliff watched the couple wander off and chat by the drink table. Eventually, they were dancing to a slow song. He didn't remember Liza being so pretty. Of course, he had all but ignored her when she lived with Ray and Jackie. He wondered where she met her French friend and if it was serious. He shook his head. What difference did it make? He reminded himself that it shouldn't. His musings were interrupted by Ray yelling at him that it was his turn at grill duty again.

The evening wore on, and families left to take their little ones home to bed. The music switched to soft ballads on the surround sound so as not to disturb the neighborhood. Pierre was ready to say his goodbyes and gushed to both Jackie and Ray about what a wonderful evening he had. Liza and Pierre walked out the side gate, and since her car was in the driveway, she drove him over a few blocks to his car. He kissed her on the cheek and said goodnight. Cliff watched Pierre and Liza leave the party hand in hand. Curiosity got the best of him, and he found Jackie sitting with her feet up. He dropped down on the grass beside her chair.

"Great party."

"It has been. And my mom hasn't let me do a thing for the last several hours."

"I saw your cousin Liza was here. She introduced me to some French guy."

"Oh, yes. Pierre. What a charming man."

"What's his story?"

"What do you mean?"

"Where did she meet him?"

"I believe he is a work associate and is a very nice guy. I didn't have much of a chance to chat, although I believe Ray talked to him at length. You might want to ask him. Liza certainly enjoys his company."

"I noticed," he mumbled.

Jackie cocked her head toward him. "Why?"

"Why what?"

"Why does it matter who he is?"

He shrugged. "It doesn't."

She smiled a knowing grin. "Uh-huh."

He popped up from the grass. "I better help Ray clean up the grills."

She was still grinning while Cliff walked off. "Interesting."

Getting home late after the party, Cliff spent several minutes thinking about Liza. Something about her puzzled him. He didn't remember her being as attractive as she appeared tonight. When he first saw her with her date, he didn't even recognize her. What happened between the day he met her so many months ago and now? She had a boyfriend, and it was too late to get to know her now. Somehow, he felt gypped, but he didn't know why. After all, he was the one who refused to date anyone. Was he changing his mind? Cliff didn't want to think about it anymore. He hit the shower and tried to wash the image of Liza down the drain.

Pierre and Liza spent much of the time together in the few weeks he was in town. The project was ending, and he made arrangements to see a few sights in the States before flying home to France. Liza helped him pick out places that were not necessarily touristy stops, but areas where he could enjoy different activities like the BBQ at Jackie's.

Jackie and Ray invited the couple over for supper more than once, and Pierre always brought some wonderful French wine to enjoy. Jackie would have to wait until after the baby was born, though, so they held off opening it until she could celebrate the birth of the baby in style. After their first supper, Jackie caught Liza alone and asked about their relationship. She laughed and whispered, "*Just friends.*" Jackie got a gleam in her eye and thought there might be a chance for Cliff yet.

"So, did you get a chance to talk to Cliff the other night at the party?"

"Well, he stopped to say hi and asked to be introduced to Pierre, but after that, we left to get drinks. Why?"

She grinned. "He asked about you later."

"I don't know why. Outside of asking how my salmon was and introducing him to Pierre, that's the only conversation I've had with him."

"Hmmm. I think he's smitten with you."

"You're crazy. Why would you think that?"

"Just a feeling I get."

Pierre interrupted to say he was ready to go home, and

Liza was glad she didn't have to respond to Jackie about Cliff. They said their goodbyes, Pierre dropped her off, and he headed for his place. He would be gone in a few days, and Liza would miss him, but he truly was just a friend. The office put on a going-away party for Pierre. He had been a great asset to the company's team, and the supervisor told him there would always be a spot for him if he wanted to stick around. They would all miss him, of course. But Liza thought it was nice to have a little male companionship, which took her by surprise. She hadn't looked at another man since her husband died.

On an occasional weekend, Jackie and Liza got together to shop for the baby. Jackie worried about how it affected Liza since she had miscarried, but Liza reminded her dear cousin that she wasn't even far enough along to realize she had been pregnant. Liza mentioned that it seemed like more of a dream. Her world crashed around her at the time, and it all seemed like one continuous nightmare. Today was her future, and she was more than happy to help Jackie shop for the little one coming at any time.

6

Liza's birthday was coming up and she had almost forgotten about it. Jackie didn't, of course, because she had been handling Liza's social calendar for the last year. They talked about going out to celebrate, but Liza wanted to have an intimate dinner at home. With Liza still not in the celebrating mood, Jackie didn't argue. Liza had come a long way-and was improving every day.

With Dr. Moline decreasing her anti-depressants, Liza was beginning to feel so much better. He explained that she was quite overmedicated, and since she hadn't returned to the doctor since her hospitalization, the dosage had never been regulated. As her life became more settled, she certainly didn't need as much medication. The current dose was now decreased to the lowest available. Liza knew that soon she would be free of her prescription, and she was also practically free from the oppressive grief from all those years ago.

Since her birthday fell on a Sunday, they decided to have supper on Saturday evening. Jackie was almost eight months along, but she insisted on cooking the meal and baking a cake. Everyone blamed it on her nesting instincts coming into play. Ray was a little worried, but Jackie shoved him out of the kitchen. She didn't even allow Liza to come early and help, and when she arrived, there were balloons, gifts, candy, and flowers. Jackie wanted to truly celebrate this year because Liza hadn't done a thing for her birthday since Jason died.

To Liza's surprise, Cliff was invited, too, and he brought a small gift. He hung out with Ray, but she felt him watching her while she set the table. Before long, everyone was handing dishes of delicious food around the table. Once everyone was eating, Cliff addressed Liza directly.

"Liza, I understand you have an apartment across town. Is it a nice building?"

Since Cliff hadn't talked to her since the BBQ, her jaw dropped open in surprise, but she was considerate enough to answer. "Yes. It's a very nice apartment. I believe the units are only a few years old."

"And where do you work?"

"Carpenter Industries." Taking another bite, she looked at Jackie, who was ignoring the whole conversation.

Ray, oblivious to her discomfort, broke into the conversation and asked Cliff about a game on TV the next day. Liza gently kicked Jackie's leg under the table and all she could do was chuckle in response. After supper, Jackie shoved Cliff and Liza into the living room and made Ray help her clean up the dishes. You didn't have to be a rocket scientist to figure out what she was doing. After settling across from each other and sitting in complete silence, Liza decided to break the ice.

"Where do you work?"

"I work for Grayson Limited as a project manager."

"And what does that entail?"

"I oversee the projects."

Liza waited for further explanations, but it didn't look like he was going to elaborate on that mundane statement.

"How long have you been there?"

"Oh, around twelve years, I guess."

"You must like it. That's a long time."

Cliff shrugged. "I guess so."

By then, Liza figured Jackie definitely lost her mind putting the two of them together in a room. "Excuse me. I'll be back."

Liza found Jackie eavesdropping, and she was laughing. Laughing! Ray looked embarrassed and practically ran out of the kitchen.

Hissing, Liza confronted her cousin. "What were you thinking?"

Jackie roared with laughter. When she was able to talk, she explained. "I've never known Cliff to be a terrible conversationalist. You've heard him with Ray. They talk non-stop. The same with me."

"This is ridiculous, Jackie. At least Pierre was interesting and could carry on a conversation."

With that, she burst out laughing again. Ray and Cliff came into the kitchen to see what was so funny, and Jackie laughed harder when she looked at their faces. Liza couldn't help herself and began to laugh, too. The men thought the ladies had lost their minds and left the room again. Several minutes later, they were calm enough to join the men. Liza opened her presents, and Cliff gave her a box of candy. Thinking how original an idea that was, she almost cracked up laughing again. Jackie evidently thought the same thing, since her lips were quivering, and she was trying to purse them tight so she wouldn't burst out in laughter again.

As soon as she could respectfully do so, Liza picked up her presents and went home, leaving Jackie to explain her laughter to Ray. Cliff left right behind her, and she managed to gracefully thank him for the candy and said goodbye.

On his drive home, Cliff berated himself for acting like an idiot. When around the table, the general conversation went fine. But the minute he addressed Liza personally, his brain went to mush. Then, when she asked him about his job, he replied with an inane answer. Liza probably figured he didn't have a brain in his head. The more he thought about the evening, the more he knew he acted like a buffoon. He talked to women all the time and never felt at a loss for words like when he was around Liza. The first time they met, he ignored her on purpose. Now that he wanted to get to know her, the words wouldn't come. At the age of thirty-two, talking to a pretty woman shouldn't be that hard.

To Jackie and Ray's delight, baby Aaron arrived on time and was perfect in every way. He was a strapping baby boy with a full head of hair. Jackie's parents arrived to spend two weeks at the house to help out with the household chores. Ray took hundreds of photos and bragged about his son to anyone who would listen. Who could blame him, after all these years of waiting?

Cliff and Liza ran into each other at her cousin's house a few times and were always cordial with one another. Over a year had passed since their first meeting, and the guy was as tongue-tied as ever around Liza. She thought it was funny and occasionally asked him a direct question to see if he could give her a decent answer. Ray gave Cliff a hard time, too. He couldn't understand Cliff's issue with not being able to have a decent conversation. Jackie would snicker and turn her attention back to Aaron.

Liza was now medication-free. Still on vitamins and exercising, she felt better than she had in years. The grief was no longer controlling her life, and remembering moments, like birthdays or holidays, were becoming bittersweet memories. Her job at Carpenter Industries was going better than she could imagine. She was already approached about a possible promotion, but she wasn't sure if she wanted the responsibility. Having only been there a year, she thought that surely there were better-qualified people to be promoted before her.

Sitting with her supervisors, Liza was asked a lot of questions, and she replied to the best of her knowledge. She stated her objections about not promoting someone else who had been at the company longer. When asked who she would suggest, she gave them two other names. They smiled and nodded, and the meeting was soon over. Figuring that was the end of the conversation, the next day she was called back into the office and offered the job anyway. Turns out, the two people that she recommended for the promotion had both recommended her for the job instead. Needless to say, Liza was flabbergasted, honored, and amazed at her future position as vice-president of special projects.

The next thing she knew, Liza was shown her own office with a view. Looking out over the city, she felt her heart suddenly speed up and tears came to her eyes as she thought of her family and Jason not being there to see how she had excelled. Brushing the tears away, she set up her laptop and organized her desk. Once that was completed, she wasn't sure what to do next. Opening the office door, she found the secretary looking back at her with a reassuring smile.

"What can I do for you, Ms. Augustine?"

Forgetting the girl's name, Liza glanced at the nameplate on her desk. Tentatively, she approached her and asked, "Carolyn, have you been in this job very long?"

"Going on six years now."

Nodding, Liza smiled back. "Good. Then you can tell me what I'm supposed to be doing."

Carolyn's smile turned into a grin as she tried not to laugh. "I believe I have your first assignment right here. I was supposed to wait until you were ready."

Blowing out a breath, Liza replied, "Thank heavens you know what I'm supposed to be doing. This is all so overwhelming."

Carolyn handed over the folder and Liza took it gratefully, held it to her chest, and then went back into her office. She left the door open this time because closing it seemed so rude. Concentrating on the information in the folder, she didn't hear her boss enter the room.

"Ms. Augustine. How do you like your office?"

Liza jumped out of her chair at the voice and banged her knee on the side of the desk. "Mr. Jackson. Hello. I was reviewing my assignment and didn't hear you come in. And yes, the office is lovely. Thank you."

"Your office door was open, so I walked in without announcing myself. I should have knocked first or had Carolyn buzz you. I apologize."

"It's fine, Mr. Jackson. This is all so new to me, I'm not sure what the protocols are yet."

"I'll give you a couple of days, then we will get our VPs together to go over everyone's new projects. They've had more time than you to prepare, so even an outline of the project will suffice this time. Once you get a handle on your needs, you can handpick your team."

"Thank you, sir. The information in the folder seems complete, so I should be ready."

He nodded and left as silently as he arrived. Carolyn

rushed in afterward and apologized.

"No problem. I expect he wanted to surprise me and see if I was dilly-dallying around or working."

"Well, it's your first day for heaven's sake." She shook her head and went back to her desk.

Liza leaned over her desk and dug into the paperwork again. Keeping this job seemed more important now than it had an hour ago. She found where she left off when Mr. Jackson scared her silly. Carolyn interrupted her thoughts sometime later.

"Ms. Augustine, it's time for me to leave. I'll see you in the morning."

Glancing at the clock, she replied, "Thank you, Carolyn. I'll see you tomorrow."

Sitting back, she stretched her arms and rotated her neck, willing to relieve the stress of the day. She got up and walked around the office, trying to decide if she should go home or stay. The building was becoming quieter by the minute. Looking out her window, she could see cars leaving the parking garage in a steady stream. Her stomach growled in protest. She had skipped lunch with all the changes. Even her eyes protested when she looked at all the paperwork on her desk. She needed to eat, or she wouldn't be able to accomplish anything else from here on out. Shuffling it all in a pile, she locked the file in her desk drawer and gathered her purse and jacket. Now that the decision was made, she shut her office door behind her and took the closest elevator down to get to her car. Instead of going home, she stopped at a small café that she favored. Once her order was placed, she leaned her head back against the booth and closed her eyes.

"May I join you?"

Peeking through one slitted eye to see who was talking to her, the shock had her sitting straight up. Standing before her was Cliff. "Uh, sure."

"Thanks. The place is full." Looking around, she wondered if she had actually dozed off for a couple of minutes. The place wasn't that full before she closed her eyes. "Hard day at work?"

Squirming in her seat, she tried to get over her embarrassment and hoped her mouth hadn't been hanging open and drooling. "Sort of."

Thankfully, the waitress brought her food and spent a couple of minutes taking Cliff's order. Liza started eating. What choice did she have? She didn't want her food to get cold while he waited for his meal to arrive. He turned his attention to her again.

He gulped, took a deep breath, and with hands wringing on his lap, Cliff said, "I can move over to the counter when a spot opens up if you'd rather."

She swallowed her food and waved her hand over the table. "This is okay if you don't mind me eating in front of you. I'm starved."

"No problem. Have at it." Cliff looked around the café and played with the saltshaker. After a couple of minutes, he said, "I'm sorry for our past meetings. For some reason, I get all tongue-tied around you and can't seem to hold an intelligent conversation. I'd like to start over."

Shrugging her shoulders, she chewed her food and mumbled, "Sure."

Cliff's food arrived, and the waitress refilled Liza's tea. Not sure where to go with this whole starting over thing, she wondered what to say, while he was stuffing his face with his burger. She finally led with a safe subject. "How long have you known Ray and Jackie?"

Cliff wiped his mouth and took a drink. "I met Ray years ago before he even knew Jackie." He paused. "How about I finish this, and we can go for a walk? It's too noisy in here, and I'd like to explain a little bit about my behavior without all these ears listening."

"I suppose that would be easier."

"Unless you need to be somewhere."

"No. No. It's just been a strange day. Please. Finish eating."

Cliff nodded and ate quickly. Paying her bill, Liza went to the parking lot to wait for Cliff. Still dressed in office attire, there was no way she was going to walk in those shoes. Scoping out a picnic table, she sat down and waited for Cliff. A couple of minutes later, he joined her.

"Don't want to walk and talk?"

"Can't. I have my work shoes on."

Cliff grinned. "Gotcha."

"So, what did you want to tell me?"

He looked over her shoulder and shook himself. Liza gave him the time he needed to gather his thoughts. He had one shot and figured he better not blow it now. He tried not to look directly at Liza so he could keep his train of thought.

"Like I said before, Ray and I met when we were freshmen in college. We became good buds, and there was a group of us that did everything together. He and I remained friends after graduation, and eventually, he married Jackie. She told me that you were her bridesmaid, but I don't remember you at all. Since I was the best man, I guess I even accompanied you down the aisle and back. She also said you were married at that time anyway." He shook his head. "Then I married a girl named Sarah. Jackie and Sarah never quite hit it off but seemed to be okay when the four of us got together. To make a long story short, Sarah and I began to have problems right away. All of a sudden, she didn't want to do anything with Ray and Jackie, and I hated her new friends. They were so snobbish. Ray and I continued doing things together, but I refused to join Sarah's friends. Then she wanted to buy this thing or that thing because her rich friends had all of this stuff. Before long, she wanted a fancy new car." Taking a deep breath, he bravely took a peek at Liza's face before continuing.

"The marriage fell apart because I refused to waste money on frivolous purchases. I gave up and went to see a lawyer. She demanded too much, and the divorce was very ugly. I found out during my filing that she had a rich boyfriend on the side, and he was happy to give her anything she wanted. Once that became known, she rubbed it in my face. But she stopped fighting me and signed the paperwork. Thankfully, we hadn't bought a house yet, nor had any children. Plus, I had refused to buy her that new car she wanted. I lost all faith in women after that, except for Jackie, of course. I tried dating a couple of times, but they weren't any nicer than Sarah. I felt completely duped by my marriage. I gave up on all dating. I haven't even been attracted to anyone all these years. Except now."

"Now?"

"When we went out for Ray's birthday, I completely ignored you. I'm sorry about being so rude, but I thought they were trying to set us up. Then I saw you at their BBQ. I didn't remember you being so pretty, and I was drawn to you. But I couldn't carry on a conversation because you always leave me speechless."

"You're certainly making up for it this evening."

Cliff shook his head. "I had a long talk with Jackie a few days ago. She told me to stop overthinking and talk to you like I do to her. I just happened to run into you tonight and made myself face my fears. Seeing you with your eyes closed, I could have left, and you would never have known I'd been there. Now I'm glad I stopped, and you were willing to listen to me."

"I can be a good listener when someone wants to actually talk. Besides, I've had my own past trauma, so I don't judge people easily. But your explanation does say a lot about your past behavior toward me."

"Whew." He looked at his watch. "I'm sorry I've taken up so much of your evening."

Yawning, Liza patted her mouth. "That's okay. It gave me time to relax, but I should go home. I have to work early in the morning."

"I'll walk you to your car."

"Cliff, one more thing."

"What is it?"

"Thank you for being a good friend to both Ray and Jackie over the years."

Smiling, Cliff nodded. "You bet. They are a great couple. And now, with Aaron, they've never been happier."

"Absolutely. I'll see you around." Getting into her car, she waved and headed for home.

Cliff stood there for a moment even after Liza was gone. Chastising himself for not making a date with her, he at least managed to talk this time. And he made sense, too. Thanks to Jackie's pep talk, he might even be able to talk to her the next time they meet.

7

Engrossed in her new position at work, Liza hadn't given Cliff much thought in the coming days. She worried more about her upcoming meeting with the boss and the other vice-presidents. Carolyn proved to be a wealth of information and explained all of the quirky personalities of some of the people she would soon be dealing with.

Along with her title of being a corporate secretary, Carolyn needed to manage an office of five. She answered calls, typed letters, scheduled trips and meetings, and did all the necessary clerical duties. Early on in her job, she made it known that she was not going to run after coffee or other errands for frivolous matters. When someone complained to her supervisor, they were told that was why they had their own coffee maker and refrigerator in their office. Carolyn also saw more than one self-important employee be demoted during her short tenure. Whoever trained her did an excellent job. Liza and Carolyn hit it off immediately.

Liza stocked her refrigerator and used one of her cupboards for snacks. It came in handy when she couldn't get away for lunch. A snack cart stopped by twice a day, but if you didn't catch it, too bad. Bringing her lunch and drinks to work was much easier than going out or to the cafeteria, and it was available when she could finally take the time to eat.

When she came into work each day, Liza left her office door open, unless she had an important call to make. The other office doors were closed all the time, and she never saw who was hiding behind those doors.

They either came in before or after her and certainly didn't welcome her to the team. If she hadn't heard someone talking to Carolyn occasionally, she would have thought she was by herself. The scheduled meeting with the boss would be the first time Liza would formally meet her co-workers. So far, she wasn't impressed.

With trepidation, Liza looked at herself in the mirror and made sure she was presentable before heading up to the meeting. She certainly wanted to give a decent presentation because she would be in front of her peers. No one asked her to go with them, and it seemed as if the group had already made up their mind about the new person. Waiting until the last minute, she got on the elevator and was by herself. Carolyn gave her words of encouragement as Liza passed by her desk.

Introductions were made, and Liza was barely acknowledged by the others in the room. She knew the attitude. These people were only out for themselves and were absolutely not team players. Her presentation was not going to be well received by them, no matter what. Thankfully, Carolyn's insight helped, and she adjusted her thoughts accordingly.

Listening attentively to the others, Liza found them arrogant and condescending to everyone in the room. She wasn't sure, but Mr. Jackson didn't look pleased, either. Finally, it was her turn. She walked with confidence to the front of the room and reached down to plug her thumb drive into the computer to begin her presentation. Laying out what the goals, needs, financial aspects, plus the end results, she explained it all with data to back up her expectations. When she was done, she pocketed the drive and sat back down. Mr. Jackson thanked her, had no questions, and dismissed the room.

"Ms. Augustine, come to my office, please."

"Of course."

Liza grabbed her notebook and file. She heard the others tittering down the hall as they left the meeting. Soon, Liza was sitting across from Mr. Jackson. A nervous wreck, she assumed her presentation was a bomb and wondered if she still had a job. She found out a few seconds later.

"I want to congratulate you on a job well done. Your presentation was flawless. I didn't expect a whole package, considering you had very little time to prepare."

She couldn't help but smile. "Thank you, sir."

"What were your thoughts on the other presentations?"

"My thoughts?"

"Yes. Did you have questions?"

"I did, but I wasn't comfortable asking since I've only been here a few days."

"I see. How about we discuss each one and you tell me what information was missing?"

"Sir, I'm not sure what you mean." Feeling uncomfortable criticizing co-workers, she squirmed in her seat.

"You had questions. So do I. They have had plenty of time to present, and they were all sorely lacking in information. I will meet with them individually later, and I'd like your input. I noticed you were making notes."

"Yes, sir, I was. It's a habit I developed over the years. It has come in handy when I've been asked to step in to assist." Liza took out her notebook and opened it to her scribbled questions.

The next two hours were spent going over each of the presentations and the information Liza felt was missing to make recommendations. Mr. Jackson was quite pleased when they were done and congratulated Liza once again on a job well done. Her project would be fully funded, and she had the go-ahead to begin setting up her team. Anyone she wanted to choose, too. She was ecstatic. Once she left Mr. Jackson's office, she knew that none of the other projects would be getting off the ground before more work was completed. Psyched, she strolled into her office, threw the presentation and notes on her desk, celebrated by punching the air, and whispered an ecstatic "*Yes!*".

Carolyn tapped on the door frame, grinning from ear to ear. "Good meeting?"

"The best. What can I do for you?"

"I thought I'd ask if there was something you needed. You looked like you were floating on air when you came by my desk. When the others returned and you didn't, I was worried. The others were gossiping about how you were in trouble already."

"I nailed my presentation. I want to thank you for your interesting tidbits ahead of time, too. It helped me tremendously when I got called into Mr. Jackson's office after the meeting."

"No problem. That's what I'm here for."

"I'm bugging out early today and going to see if my cousin is available for a visit. Tomorrow, I'll be setting up my team and I'll need a lot of help from you."

"I'll be ready. Of course, I will need to divide my time with the others."

Giving her a sly smile she said, "That's not going to be a problem tomorrow. See you later."

Leaving the office, she couldn't help but be ecstatic about how her day went. When she got to her car, she called Jackie. Telling her to head straight over, Liza was ready to get a little Aaron-time. She also had a hankering for pizza and convinced Jackie to let her order in for supper, timing it for when Ray would be home from work. In the meantime, Jackie, Aaron, and Liza had a wonderful time together while they waited. She was even allowed to change a diaper. They were discussing whether Jackie was going to go back to work or not when the pizza arrived, followed shortly by Ray. Timing is everything when it comes to hot pizza.

While Jackie fed Aaron, and with Ray still chowing down on pizza, Liza sat back sated and happy. She had so enjoyed the visit and was glad she ended her day with her cousin. Excited to tell them about her week, she waited until Ray was done eating.

"Okay, Cuz. Spit it out. You have been hiding something since you got here today."

Grinning, Liza was practically bursting at the seams to talk. "I got a promotion at work and was given only a couple of days to prepare my presentation for my first assigned project. I nailed it and the big boss called me to my office to congratulate me on a great job."

They praised her effusively, and then Jackie asked, "Why didn't you call me right away after you were offered the promotion?"

"First, I didn't think I should have one already since I haven't been there as long as some others. But they gave it to me anyway. Then I was assigned a project right out of the gate, and I knew it would be a make or break. I guess I needed to do this to prove to myself I could do it, but if I didn't, no one else would know. I didn't want the sympathy card played again. I'm trying to take responsibility for my life, you know."

Jackie shook her head. "Silly girl. I'm going to lay

Aaron down. I'll be right back."

Ray went to the den to watch TV, taking the last of the pizza with him. Liza cleaned up the kitchen while waiting for Jackie to return. She fixed them both a fresh drink and sat at the center island to wait.

When Jackie came back into the kitchen Liza said, "Guess who I ran into earlier in the week? Or should I say, ran into me?"

"Who?"

"Cliff."

Jackie's eyes lit up. "Really? Where at? How did that go? What did he say?"

Laughing at the interrogation, she shook her head. "I was at Charlie's Café, sitting there with my eyes closed. He stopped and asked if he could join me because the place was packed, which I agreed to. I got my food right afterward and started to eat. We didn't say much, but Cliff said he wanted to talk to me. He also said you two visited the other day."

"We did. Continue." She leaned forward in anticipation.

"We went outside after he was done eating. He asked me to do a walk and talk, except I was in my work shoes. I found an empty picnic table, instead. He told me about his ex and how he became disillusioned with women. Except you. He has compared all other women to you and your relationship with Ray."

"That man stands by his friends. Sarah wasn't always a snob. Not early on. Her parents are really nice people. Anyway, we got along for several months, but she always wanted more. Then she found a group of rich, snobby women and some rich guy that she got on the hook. I'm glad Cliff got out of there when he did."

"I told him that was the most I'd ever heard him talk

unless it was to Ray."

"He just needed to break the ice. When are you seeing him again?"

"I don't know. We didn't set up a date or anything. He cleared the air and that was about it."

"Oh. I figured he would ask you out. You would go, wouldn't you?"

Shrugging, Liza contemplated the question. "I don't know. I hadn't given it any thought. We got off to a bad start, so it's not like I feel anything for him."

"Well, I still think he is smitten with you, so give it a try."

"No harm in making a friend, even though we could have been friends over a year ago if he hadn't been such an idiot." Jackie roared with laughter at her response. "I had a good time with Pierre while he was here. He turned out to be a great friend. I miss his ideas at work. I wonder if I can get him to come back and stay?"

"That would make Cliff very jealous."

"Jealous? Why?"

"You should have seen him that night at the BBQ. Cliff couldn't keep his eyes off of you. Once he heard Pierre's accent, he worried that he'd blown his chance with you."

"All the single girls had a great time flirting with Pierre. I bet a couple of the married ones did, too."

"Nothing like a Frenchman to bring out the giddiness in the ladies. Anyway, are you serious about Pierre?"

"Just as a friend and co-worker. The company offered him a job if he wanted to stay, but I think he has a special someone at home."

"Ah." Aaron whimpered and fussed. "Sounds like I need to change a diaper or something."

"It's late. I'll head for home then and say goodbye to Ray on my way out."

"Thanks for the pizza. It was nice to not have to cook for a change."

"Anytime." They hugged and parted ways.

8

The ringing phone woke Jackie up. "Hello?"

"Jackie. It's Cliff. Did I wake you?"

"Yeah, but it's probably a good thing. I hear Aaron on the monitor, fussing. I'd rather get to him before he begins wailing."

"I guess I'm good for something."

"What did you need?"

"Liza's number."

"Sure. Let me take care of the little guy first, then I'll text it to you."

"Thanks, Jackie. You're the best."

"I know. Don't break her heart." She hung up before he could respond.

Several minutes later, his phone pinged with Liza's number. Then it took several more minutes before he was brave enough to make the call. After he finally got up the nerve, the call ended up in her voicemail.

"Hi. It's Cliff. Jackie gave me your number. I hope that is all right. Give me a call back when you have a chance. I'd like to set up a day when we can go out together. If you're interested, that is. Okay. Thanks. Bye."

He shook his head and thought how dumb he sounded. He wouldn't blame her if she didn't return his call. He looked at the clock and assumed she was still at work, and it might be some time before she got back to him. Instead of pacing the floor, Cliff decided to start some laundry and do his dishes. Anything to stay busy.

*****

Liza walked out of her last meeting for the day and dropped her folders and notebooks on the desk. Her laptop was on top of the stack, and it almost slid off to the floor. Catching it in time, she laid it aside, then took a deep breath. The assignments were handed out, and the team would meet on Monday morning, bright and early. Exhausted, she was still able to feel proud of the job she had done so far. Mr. Jackson popped in and observed a couple of times but would just nod before leaving. She took that as a positive note. Now, it was dark outside, and all she wanted to do was go home to bed. Grabbing her purse, she shut the office door behind her. The next thing she knew, she was crawling into bed, curling up, and promptly fell asleep.

*****

Cliff looked at the clock and decided Liza wasn't going to call him back. The house was clean, and he had nothing left to do except shower and go to bed. Disappointment rolled over him, but he almost felt like he deserved not to get a return call. After all, he ignored and avoided her for almost a year. Sighing, he did the only thing he could do for now. Go to bed.

*****

Liza slept in until almost ten. When she sat up on the side of the bed, she knew why. She was sick. Barely making it to the bathroom before everything she ate the evening before made its presence known, she didn't know if it was food poisoning or the flu. But either way, she went back to bed. Around four, she heard pounding on her door and realized Jackie was yelling. By the time Liza let her in, she was sure the whole building was outraged. Jackie barged in, took one look at her, and stopped yelling. Taking stock of her disheveled look and the terrible smell made her worry instead of being mad or scared. She couldn't make up her mind which. Liza made it to the couch and collapsed.

"What happened?"

"I'm sick." Lying there with her eyes closed, Liza couldn't stand the spinning of the room.

"No kidding. I can tell that. What is it? Will I take it home to Aaron? Maybe I should leave. But you need help. I don't know what to do. Tell me what you need."

Managing to mumble out a few words, Liza kept her eyes closed. "Maybe something to drink. Electrolytes. I don't have a fever, so it's probably food poisoning. I don't know if anyone else got sick."

"Where's your phone? It keeps going straight to voicemail. I thought you were dead or something."

"Purse."

Jackie dug through her purse and turned the phone on. Soon, it was pinging with notifications and messages. "Unlock your phone and I'll see if there is anything important besides me trying to call you all day." Liza managed to open one eye long enough to see the phone and unlock it. She handed it back and closed her eyes again. "Let's see. Me. Me. Me. Me. A bunch of me's. Mr. Jackson. Somebody named Carrie, and Cliff.

"Are there voicemails?"

"Hmmm. Looks like it."

"Put it on speaker and start with Mr. Jackson."

Jackie clicked on his call. He said she was doing an excellent job, and that he would see her on Monday. Next was Carrie, she was sick and thought it was the food. She didn't know if anyone else got sick or not. Cliff's message was a surprise, and she had Jackie play it twice.

Squinting up at Jackie, she asked, "You gave him my number?"

"It's not like he's a mass murderer, you know."

"That's fine. Would you text him that I'm sick and will get back to him in a couple of days?"

"Sure." Jackie smiled as she whipped out a message.

"Done. Now. I'll go get you some stuff to make you feel better. I'll leave the door unlocked so I can get back in. When I return, I'll help you get in the shower."

"I'm sorry I never got you a spare key. I keep forgetting to have one made."

"No problem. You'll get me one eventually."

Liza continued to doze while Jackie went shopping. A shower did sound good, but she was awfully weak. Soon, Jackie was blowing back through the door, talking the whole time. Liza couldn't help but laugh inside. That poor girl needed to get out more. She probably talked to herself the whole time she was at the store. Now she was helping her sit up and drink something. Whatever it was, it was cold and sweet, but it certainly helped quench her thirst. Soon, she was standing under a hot shower, and Liza finally felt like she might live.

Once she got out of the shower, Liza put on the clean jammies that Jackie left out for her, then padded to the kitchen. Jackie had already changed her bedding, and the washer was running. Dishing up a bowl of soup, she put some crackers on the side and placed it in front of her. Jackie was still talking non-stop, and Liza didn't bother interrupting. When Jackie finally ran out of steam, Liza was done eating.

"Thank you for everything. I feel so much better."

She handed over a drink container. "This has more of the electrolytes you need. I bought more soup and drinks, so take care of yourself this weekend."

"I'll be okay now. As long as I can keep all of this down, I should be on the mend."

"Great. Don't forget to call Cliff back."

"Sure. In a couple of days. I'll have to see how my Monday at work goes, and how many of my employees got sick."

"Who made the food?"

"I don't know. I'll have my secretary check into it."

"Well, I'm outta here. Ray is watching Aaron so who knows what's happening at home."

Still tired but not feeling as sick, Liza was ready to go back to bed. Picking up her phone, she locked the door and then shut off the lights on the way to the bedroom. Snuggling into her clean sheets, she closed her eyes. Surprisingly, she slept all night but felt all but normal when she awakened the following morning. Remaining in her pj's all day, she rested. Her mind seldom thought about work, and that was a first. She was still too tired to care about much of anything.

On Monday morning, her team dragged themselves into the conference room. Pete looked terrible and argued whether or not he needed to see his doctor. Finally agreeing when Liza threatened to call an ambulance, he left, only to be admitted to the hospital later that day. The rest of the crew were lucky.

Carolyn checked where the food was obtained and quickly found out that other meeting-goers were also affected. The food prep company turned itself in to the health department, and it was closed down until the source was recognized. They also needed to figure out how and why the company didn't know they were serving contaminated food. By Tuesday, almost everyone that had gotten sick was back to normal. Pete wasn't as lucky and would be gone for several days.

Finally calling Cliff back on Monday evening, they set up a Saturday afternoon outing. Nothing special, but if the weather was good, they would take a walk in the park. They both knew that they needed to get to know each other. Too bad he hadn't taken that opportunity months ago. Liza still wasn't sure why she was going to see him, but Jackie encouraged her to at least be his friend. And she did promise to do that much.

Jason had been gone for several years now, and Liza hadn't so much as looked at another man. There was so much grief and despair for so many months running, it hadn't even occurred to her. Right now, she was involved in work and wasn't sure she had the time or energy to build a relationship with anyone. But she would do anything that Jackie asked her to do.

9

Prairie Park had great walking trails, and Liza and Cliff agreed to meet in the parking lot that Saturday. He was already waiting for her when she pulled up, and she was even a little early.

"You made it."

"Did you think I wouldn't?"

"Not exactly. I mean, I hoped you would." He tried to muffle a groan.

"Well, I'm here. Which trail did you want to take?"

"Do you have a favorite?"

"Probably Excalibur."

"Excalibur it is. Let's go."

Grabbing a backpack that held a supply of water and snacks, Liza threw it on and looked over at Cliff. "Don't you have a water bottle?"

"I forgot to bring extra, and I already drank the one I had in my car while waiting for you. I'll be fine. Do you want me to carry the backpack?"

"Nope. I got it. Lead on."

Walking in silence for the first half mile or so, Cliff finally spoke. "You must be feeling better if you're up to this trail."

"One hundred percent."

"They ever figure out what made everyone sick?"

"Yeah. It was the pasta salad. The mayo was bad. Real bad. But it didn't ruin the taste of the salad, so I guess that's why we all ate it. I think they said something about contamination. Even the guy that made it got sicker than a dog."

"Wow. That's too bad."

"Turns out, there's a recall on the product and it wasn't something that the caterers did. I hope they can recover their business from the incident."

"Sounds like that could financially ruin them."

"Could be. I don't know much more than that."

After several minutes, Cliff changed the subject. "Tell me about your job."

"I recently got a promotion. Technically, I'm vice-president of special products development."

"Wow. When did you get that job?"

"The company surprised me with it a couple of weeks ago. I had to hit the ground running. My first test was to show I was competent, a couple of days after I was given the job. I had to lay out how I would advance the project I was handed. My boss is impressed. Not so much with some others on my floor. I think they've gotten lazy or sloppy over the past few months."

"Really?"

"Not my problem. They are arrogant and expect others to bow to their almighty presence."

"Whoa. Not impressed much, huh?"

"Nope. Not my monkeys, not my zoo." Cliff broke out laughing and she couldn't help but join in. "So, you are a project manager, too, right?"

"Yip. Grayson Industries provides construction materials for anything you might need. Say someone is building or remodeling a house. We will help the owner decide on the interior products, then follow through and have them installed. Same with commercial properties. We have an outdoor division, but I only handle indoor projects."

"Do you draw the sketches up and everything?"

"Yes. I do all the initial visits and drawings, then once the owner agrees to the options, I get a team together to make the magic happen."

"Sounds like an interesting job. Always something new going on that way."

Noticing they were at the halfway mark, the couple stopped at the overlook which gave them a three-hundred-and-sixty-degree view of the city. Dropping the backpack on a bench, Liza dug out two water bottles and packages of trail mix.

"Here." She handed over half the goodies.

"Thanks. At least one of us was prepared." Grinning, Liza popped more trail mix in her mouth, while Cliff blushed about his lack of preparation for a long hike. "Do you feel like telling me about your past? All Jackie ever said was you have lost most of your family."

Picking up the backpack, throwing away the trash, and finishing their waters, they moved on. "I will give you the condensed version. I lost everyone within a short span of time. My husband, Jason, died in a pileup on the interstate, then I miscarried. Shortly after, my parents died from carbon monoxide poisoning. Then a few months later, my brother died from an IED overseas. I zoned out for several months, but Jackie came to my rescue. Eventually, I moved in with her and Ray, and she took care of me. That's when you met me for the first time. I'd probably still be floundering if she hadn't convinced me to stay with her."

"I knew she was your cousin."

"Yes. We've known each other forever. When we were kids and got together, we were quite the little hoodlums."

"I can believe that of her, but I don't see that in you."

Chuckling, she shook her head. "She brings it out in me. Besides, you have to have a leader and a follower to make things work properly."

They hiked the rest of the way and spent more time looking at the view than talking. By the time they got back to their cars, the couple agreed to meet for supper. But first, a shower was called for. Cliff would stop and pick her up in two hours and Liza said she would meet him out in front of the apartments.

They decided to go to Charlie's. Casual, yet the atmosphere lent to the ability of friendly conversation most of the time. Plus, the food was great. Still early, they had their choice of tables. Surprisingly for a Saturday night, the café wasn't busy yet. Taking advantage of a table in the back, they ordered and then visited about a myriad of things. Finishing his meal, Cliff pushed his empty plate aside and looked over at Liza.

"You know, that first night at Ray's birthday party, you looked different than when I saw you later at the BBQ. I still can't figure it out."

Finishing her last bite, Liza sat back. "I was a mess. Jackie made an appointment for me with her doctor, and we began to back off my anti-depressants. I'd been on a very high dose for three years without a dosage adjustment. The high dose was making my head pretty fuzzy, but I didn't realize it at the time. Dr. Moline felt that I could work my way down to a lower level. Jackie had me on a full regimen of vitamins and minerals, then fixed great meals to fatten me up. Being with her all the time certainly gave me the strength to begin to cope with life once again. Anyway, it turns out I was overmedicated. My fault entirely for not returning to the doctor for appointments. And the doctor just kept refilling the prescription. I guess he figured I must have been doing fine on the dosage he prescribed, or I would have gone back. To make a long story short, we continued to decrease the dosage each month until I got off them completely. Turns out my depression was considered situational, not clinical. Plus, I needed to deal with the grief process, and I couldn't do it all drugged up like I was. Through all of this, Jackie was the key. She brought me out of my funk and made me get healthy again. We walked and talked, and she was probably better than any therapist I had ever gone to. By the time you saw me at the BBQ, I was healthier and felt more self-assured. I got a job, have good friends, and love from the only family I have left. Jackie's parents stepped up when I needed them, too, even though my aunt was grieving her sister."

"That would make sense. You were pretty withdrawn and mousy-looking that first night. But I probably didn't help matters by ignoring you all those months."

"Well, you were pretty much rude to me, but at that point, I didn't care. Both Jackie and I thought it was funny about you being scared to talk to me."

Cliff blushed again. He certainly embarrassed easily. "Sorry. I still don't know why I couldn't have a decent conversation with you. At first, I wasn't interested and thought they were throwing us together. Then when you piqued my interest, I was too tongue-tied. As Jackie said, just talk to you like a friend, and that seems to have finally done the trick."

"I guess so. You haven't stopped talking since."

"Hey. You are kind of intimidating now."

"Say what?" Liza's eyes grew wide.

"I mean, now you seem so self-assured, and here I am, still bumbling around."

"Looks can be deceiving, Cliff." All she heard in response was a quiet "*Hmmm*." When they pulled up to the apartment building, Liza stopped Cliff from getting out. "It's okay. I can find my way to my apartment."

He hesitated. "I'm sure you can, but I thought it a gentlemanly thing to do to open the car door and walk you to your place."

"I'm good. Thanks for a wonderful day. We'll have to do this again sometime."

"Next Saturday?"

"Call me in a few days and I'll see how my work schedule goes."

Cliff sighed, and his shoulders drooped. "Okay."

He looked devastated. "One step at a time, Cliff. We're now officially friends, right?"

"Right."

Liza stepped out of the car and gave him a wave before entering the building. She reminded herself as she opened the door to her apartment, life is just one step at a time.

10

Because her office door was open most of the time, Liza heard the comings and goings of the other people on their part of the floor. Carolyn worked for five vice-presidents, and sometimes she wasn't treated well. If Liza heard someone being condescending, she would go to her doorway and look out. The individual realized they were being watched and would sometimes tone down their voice or just go back into their hidey-hole. Usually, it was the same guy causing grief. She never did like him from the moment they were introduced.

That day, Liza heard someone stomp through the hall, muttering and cursing, yelling at Carolyn for a file, and then slamming his door. Never remembering the guy's name, she knew exactly who was making noise. Having several phone calls to make, she shut her door so as not to be disturbed. Soon, she was involved in a lengthy conversation when there began a commotion outside her door. It was so loud that the person on the other end of the line was concerned. Apologizing, Liza promised to call back after she checked on the problem. Paging security before she even went to her door, she peeked out to see what the issue was. Mr. Intolerable was throwing papers and files all over the room and screaming at Carolyn, who was rightfully cowering behind her desk. In her hand was a letter opener for protection. The other VPs were either hiding in their office or doing a little peeking of their own.

Slowly, Liza opened her door enough to walk through and get to Carolyn. Leading the scared woman into her office, Liza made sure her back was never turned toward the angry man. She soon closed the door and locked it behind them. Helping Carolyn sit down, she collapsed and took a big breath.

"What is going on out there?"

"He's crazy."

"I can see that."

Carolyn took some shuddering breaths. "I took him the file he requested, and the next thing I know he's screeching, cursing, and throwing files all over the room."

Hearing a scuffle outside the door, they heard Mr. Intolerable screaming to be let go. Unlocking the office, Liza took a peek to see that the security guys had pinned him to the floor and zip-tied his hands behind his back. The guy was bucking like a banshee, too. Mr. Jackson arrived to supervise the situation and had already called the local police for assistance. In the meantime, security planned to sit on him until they arrived. Literally.

When Mr. Jackson saw Liza standing in her doorway, he looked around the room. No other door was open except hers. He walked across the mess to her office, skirting file after file to get there. She invited him inside, shut the door against the noise, and Mr. Jackson walked over to a now bawling Carolyn. The poor girl was still gripping the letter opener. He finally got her to loosen her hold and took the opener from her, laying it on Liza's desk, far away from Carolyn. She finally looked around and realized she was safe. Taking a deep shaky breath, she wiped her eyes, blew her nose, and told Mr. Jackson she was okay.

"I think I had a delayed reaction is all." She could still hear the commotion out in the other room.

Mr. Jackson sat beside her. "You're safe now.

Security has him pinned down and the police are coming. I'll press charges for assault and destruction of property. Did he hurt you?"

"No." She took another breath.

"I can call an ambulance if you are."

Carolyn's eyes grew wide. "Oh, no, sir. He didn't hit me because I moved too fast and went behind my desk. He verbally threatened me. Then he began throwing papers around and tearing apart the filing cabinets. I don't know what's the matter with him, sir."

"It sounds to me like he's having a psychotic break. If you're okay, I'll let Ms. Augustine stay with you. I hear the officers now." She nodded her head.

Liza got out two bottles of water and they sat together and drank. With the door now open, they could see the officers hauling Mr. Intolerable out of the office. One of the officers stayed behind and took statements. Mr. Jackson called his secretary after the police left so she could help pick up and organize the files. All this time, the other VPs stayed within their four walls and didn't bother to help anyone. Whoever was watching Mr. Intolerable tear the office apart disappeared when Mr. Jackson arrived on the scene. Once it was calm again, they opened their doors, took pictures of the mess, and talked among themselves. That is until Mrs. Carney arrived from Mr. Jackson's office. Then, just like the moles that they were, they hid back in their offices. Appalled at their behavior, Liza offered to help.

"Mrs. Carney, may I help you?"

"I don't know. This appears to be quite the mess, doesn't it?"

Looking around, Liza said, "That's an understatement." It looked like one of the filing cabinets was emptied and spread everywhere.

Carolyn came out of the office and choked out, "Good lord. This is so much worse than I thought it would be."

Worried about the poor girl, Mrs. Carney asked, "Carolyn, don't you want to go home?"

She threw back her shoulders and looked everyone right in the eye. "Absolutely not. But we could use all the help we can get. Let's set up a long table over by that wall so we can sort the papers and files into piles."

Liza smiled and felt that she couldn't have had more respect for Carolyn than right then. The three of them set up the table and got to work. By the time Mr. Jackson returned, they had a small corner cleaned.

"You three are doing this yourselves?"

They nodded and kept concentrating on the papers they were sorting. He went to another area and picked up a few files and went to work. Two hours later, they had everything organized, and Mrs. Carney and Carolyn were refiling everything into the cabinet. Mr. Jackson looked around the room to make sure they didn't miss anything.

"Very good." Then he yelled with his hands cupped around his mouth and made sure it was loud enough for everyone hiding in their offices to hear. "Olly-olly-oxen free!" He stood there waiting. The doors began opening, as Carolyn, Mrs. Carney, and Liza stood in shock. They stared at their boss for yelling out a childhood game. "So. You are all hiding out. I suspected as much. March up to my office. Now."

The VPs looked at each other, then took off. But not before giving Liza a dirty look. She shrugged and went back to her office. Seeing the letter opener, Liza took it back to Carolyn's desk and said, "Don't lose this. You never know when you'll need it to slice something open."

Carolyn's mouth dropped open, then she cracked up laughing, followed by Liza joining in. Soon, Mr. Jackson joined in their laughter before heading up to his office.

Mrs. Carney looked at them all and shook her head. "What am I missing?" Which made Carolyn and Liza laugh all the harder.

Liza went back to her office to make the call that was so rudely interrupted earlier. She gently shut her door and went back to work. Carolyn went home long before Liza did, and no one knew what happened to the other VPs. They weren't going to like her any better after today. Realizing how tired she was, Liza couldn't wait to go home. She soaked in a hot tub of water while eating a sandwich. She always was a multi-tasker.

Three days after the manic episode at the office, everyone found out that Nathan, or Mr. Intolerable, was committed instead of being jailed. He was high on drugs, and whatever they were, had sent him over the edge. A couple of weeks previous, his wife filed for divorce. Nathan not only ruined his family life but his career, too. Carolyn didn't feel sorry for him after she was terrorized by the guy. She had been dealing with his steadily increasing behaviors on a daily basis. No one blamed her. After all, she was the one defending herself with a letter opener.

The other VPs were reprimanded, and one was insistent that he wasn't about to be involved in other people's drama. Shortly thereafter, he was demoted back to his old job. Everyone assumed he would be quitting as soon as he found another job. The other two agreed to straighten up and quit thinking they were better than everybody else, or they could follow their co-worker. No one wanted to be demoted, and they had to swallow their pride. Now when Liza said hello, they answered back. One even started to leave her door open occasionally. Life is funny that way.

Liza begged off her Saturday date with Cliff, saying that her week had been too long and involved. But they did plan to meet Sunday afternoon at Jackie and Ray's place. Games were on TV, and Liza even wanted to watch one of them. She enjoyed being around others as they rooted for their teams. Besides, she was for the opposite team than Cliff, so she thought it might be pretty interesting to see how that worked out.

Ballgames, food, drinks, and laughter are all it takes for a good time. And of course, real friends. Liza's team won, which gave her bragging rights, until at least the following weekend. She left the house with her head held high and went home to chill before facing another week at work. She hoped it wasn't nearly as adventurous as the week before. The project team was awesome, and they were ahead of schedule. Mr. Jackson was well pleased with the weekly updates. Liza was feeling more confident in her position and couldn't wait to see what the boss had in store for them next.

Cliff asked Liza to go to a Saturday matinée, where he was introduced to animated cartoons. He couldn't believe he enjoyed the movie as much as he did. There would be no walking that day as there was a light drizzle. So, keeping with the theme of the day, they went to the indoor arcade and played mini-golf, and rode the go-karts, where she won both contests. Cliff was left checking his manhood at the door, and Liza wanted to make sure he could remain friends with a strong independent woman.

Sitting across from Liza at McDonald's, both eating a kid's meal, Cliff couldn't help but admire her. She was nothing like Jackie. With Liza continually surprising him, he was becoming more enamored with her every day. Laughing at their tiny meals, they were still hungry, so he bought them a sundae to end the night. Luckily, the ice cream machine was working. He couldn't wait for their next date.

"I know you don't like to plan too far in advance, but when can I see you again?"

Taking her last bite of ice cream, she pondered the question. "Well, how about Wednesday? I can meet you at Charlie's after work."

"Your work time or mine?" he grinned.

"How about I text you when I get ready to leave the office?"

"Perfect."

Cliff dropped Liza off and headed straight over to Ray's place. Okay, it was Jackie he wanted to see, but he supposed Ray would be there hanging around. Cliff barged in as soon as Ray opened the door.

"Hey, Buddy. How was your date?"

"Good. Is Jackie around?"

"Yeah. She's bathing Aaron in the kitchen sink. Something wrong?"

"Not a thing."

Ray scratched his head. "Okay." They headed to the kitchen and sat at the counter.

Jackie looked up and reached for a towel. "You just missed splash-a-rama time." She looked drenched.

Cliff laughed. "Hey. Look at you, little guy."

Jackie wrapped Aaron tight in a big fluffy towel and handed him off to Cliff. "You hold him. I need to change my shirt – again." She was soon back and reached for Aaron. "I need to get him dressed before he gets cold."

"Jackie, I just wanted to thank you for your encouragement where Liza is concerned."

"You're welcome. Things going well, then?"

"So far. She's an amazing woman. I didn't expect to find a new dimension every time we are together."

She smiled, then became serious. "Liza is not only my cousin but my best friend. I will personally kill you if you hurt her."

He backed away, holding his hands up in front of him. "We are taking it slow and building a friendship. Now, I'll get out of here and let you get back to Aaron."

Cliff took off and Ray threw his arm over Jackie's shoulder as they walked to Aaron's room. "Their relationship sounds promising after all."

"I know. She deserves some happiness in her life."

"So does Cliff. It's been so long since he's had someone. Now that we have Aaron, I notice it more."

Jackie gave Ray a quick kiss on the nose and handed him his now fully dressed son. "I'll fix a bottle, and you can feed and put him to bed tonight."

"You got it."

Jackie took a shower and checked on her favorite men. They were still playing, so she grabbed her phone to text Liza. "If you aren't too tired, call." Her phone rang immediately. "Hey, girl."

"How's my favorite cousin?"

"Great. We're all great."

"Good, what's up?"

"We just had a quick visit from Cliff. He thanked me for helping approach you again."

Liza chuckled. "I guess I should thank you for encouraging me to give him a chance."

"Things are going okay?"

"I consider him a friend, but that's all right now."

"That's a start, I guess."

"It's good to enjoy male company again, but he's not Jason."

"And you aren't anywhere close to being Sarah. I didn't know Jason well, but I know he was good to you. Sarah, on the other hand, was a witch. And that's being nice."

"I hope I never run into her."

"Doubtful. I think she and her sugar daddy moved out of town."

"Change of subject. Do you need a day out soon?"

"Absolutely. I've been interviewing babysitters, but I'm not happy with anyone."

"Have you given any thought about not going back to work?"

"Lots. Ray and I go back and forth on the subject, but he says it is ultimately up to me."

"We'll talk about it when I see you next. What day works for you?"

"I get groceries on Saturday morning, so I'll see if Ray will be home in the afternoon."

"You can bring Aaron, you know."

"I know, but I have to take so much stuff with me. I'll get back to you in a couple of days once I check with Ray. His parents are out of town for a few weeks, so I can't even ask them to help right now."

"Okay. You got it. I'll hold Saturday afternoon open for now."

"Good. Night, Cuz."

"Goodnight."

11

Cliff enjoyed his Wednesday evening outings with Liza. This week, she told him a slightly exaggerated tale of Nathan's enormous fit at the office. No names, of course, along with no other personal details, but a week after the incident, it was quite a tale to fabricate a bit. He didn't have any story nearly as funny to tell, but they had a marvelous time anyway. The couple made it a routine to meet at Charlie's and sat at the same table every time. They tried to meet up again on the weekend, but this coming Saturday, Liza had plans with Jackie. Cliff was just going to have to wait until the following week to see her again. After eating, they often took walks. Liza carried a pair of casual shoes in the car for these situations. They had already come in handy several times. The weather began turning cooler, and fall was approaching, so many times a jacket was also required.

Liza was moving forward with her second project, and her team was the best she had ever worked with. Mr. Jackson promoted someone to take Nathan's spot, but not without Liza's approval first. She knew the staff and who deserved to be recognized. Now, she and Casey Sharpton collaborated and had the highest output in the whole company.

Liza's quarterly bonus was well-earned, and those on her team were also compensated well. After Carolyn's run-in with Nathan, Mr. Jackson gave her a healthy pay increase, too. He told her it was battle pay. Liza bragged about how Carolyn ran her office with an iron fist and knew more about the business than anyone on their floor. She deserved every dime of her raise.

Hikes with Cliff were more sporadic due to the weather, but they would fit them in on a Saturday or Sunday almost every week. Three months after the couple began seeing each other regularly, Cliff and Liza found themselves sitting together looking at the full moon. Halloween was in a couple of days, and the moon was perfectly timed for the holiday. As if in mutual agreement, the two turned and looked at each other adoringly, then kissed. It wasn't long, but meaningful for them both. Cliff enveloped Liza in his arms and held her for several moments. When he leaned back, he could see tears welling up in her eyes. He was a little overwhelmed himself.

Pulling her back in a hug for a moment, they silently looked at the moon again. Cliff walked Liza to her door for the first time, kissed her again, then left her standing in her open doorway. She smiled dreamily as she leaned against her now shut door, touching her swollen, just kissed lips. She felt amazing. Locking her door, she felt like she was a teenager all over again.

Cliff managed to get to his car without falling down the steps. He wasn't sure if Liza felt like he did right now, but he hoped so. The next thing he knew, he was pulling into his driveway. Smiling, he managed to get into the house without tripping over his own two feet.

Time flew by, and Christmas was arriving. Liza wasn't sure she was ready to celebrate another holiday. This was the second one she would celebrate since feeling human again. With Jackie's help, she managed to get through the whole holiday season the year before without a relapse. No parents, no brother, and no husband. The pain was real, and the grief was almost overwhelming at times, but she wondered if it was her way of dealing with the loss of her family. She hadn't dealt with it before and had turned her emotions in on herself. Being overmedicated hadn't helped at all.

Jackie and Ray would be having Christmas at their house with her parents arriving to stay for a few days. Cliff was going to his parents' home. He asked Liza if she would come with him, but she felt it was way too soon in their blossoming relationship to make that trip. Besides, her Christmas blues usually got in the way. He had years to get over Sarah, and it was time for Liza to work through her own demons. If she was to move forward with Cliff, or anyone for that matter, she needed to leave her past behind her where it belonged.

Liza took Cliff to her corporate Christmas party, and she wondered if he was going to skip out more than once. Evidently, he was quite overwhelmed. The last straw was when Mr. Jackson stopped by, called out her name, and slapped Cliff on the back. His company's party was the following week, and she would be subjected to the same thing, only on a smaller scale. Except his boss would ignore Cliff and Liza, which he was grateful for. His introverted personality was certainly in full force around crowds. Now it made more sense as to why it took so long for him to talk to Liza in a casual conversation.

Christmas was on a Thursday, and both of their companies planned to close until after the New Year. It gave everyone a forced vacation and time to see family and recoup. They planned to get together for their usual Wednesday night at Charlie's for their own Christmas celebration, then go to Liza's apartment to exchange gifts. Liza couldn't decide what to buy him but eventually found a jersey of his favorite football player. Too bad he still liked the wrong team. They agreed on a price ahead of time so they could make sure they didn't overspend each other and kept it simple.

On New Year's Eve, along with Jackie and Ray, the group had dinner reservations for a night on the town. Jackie's parents planned to stay from Christmas through the New Year celebrations to give everyone a chance to go out. The meal was great, and the dancing afterward was special. Liza hadn't enjoyed a night out like that for years. In fact, her whole holiday season turned out better than she ever expected.

Lying in bed the following morning, she thought about the last month. Outside of her earlier dreading of the holiday season, she handled them all pretty well and believed she was ready to move forward with Cliff. She picked up the necklace he gave her for Christmas. It looked like a diamond, but he assured her it wasn't. Taking more than one long look, she still wasn't convinced that a real diamond wasn't in the center of the setting.

Today, she planned on being lazy and didn't have to be back to work until Monday. Cliff was going back on Friday. It seemed silly that his company didn't just give them that extra day off, but she wasn't going to fret over something she couldn't control.

Looking in the mirror, Liza wasn't sure she recognized the person that stared back. Her features had changed so much over the last couple of years. For the good, thankfully. She thought back to when she first moved into Jackie's place, and again when she moved into the apartment. It was all night and day, with the changes in her life. Her maternal clock was ticking, and if her relationship with Cliff didn't work out, she would have to assume she would never have a baby of her own. Shaking her head, she jumped in the shower, trying to wash her self-doubts away. She still had a fantastic job at a great company. So, there was that.

12

The weeks were flying by, and spring was just around the corner. Liza took every chance she got to hike at the park just around the corner from her apartment. Cliff was alluding to a permanent long-term relationship, and Liza was unconsciously pulling her emotions back. In fact, she believed he was going to ask her to marry him, and it scared her to death. She couldn't make heads or tails of how she was feeling about him, either. One day she was madly in love, the next she was running scared.

Jackie finally chose to quit her job and loved staying home with Aaron. He was getting so big, and Liza enjoyed the time she got to spend with the family. She wanted that happiness for herself, so she couldn't figure out why she was running away from the possibility. Even Jackie knew something was wrong. One evening, she pulled Liza out the patio door for a private talk.

"Tell me what's happening between the two of you."

Pacing in front of her, Liza shook her head. "I wish I knew. Things are going so well between us, I guess I'm just scared."

"Of what?"

"About committing to him, and then how I'd feel if I lost him like I did Jason."

"Oh, Liza. You never know about tomorrow. You know that. We have no control over car accidents like Jason's. Cliff is head over heels with you. I was worried about you getting hurt, but I can see it might be the other way around." Jackie threw up her hands. "Sit down. You're pacing is driving me nuts."

"I'm sorry." They sat on the porch swing and began rocking.

"Look. Do you love Cliff or are you in love with the thought of having love again?"

Liza sat back and stared at the darkening sky. "I don't know. I'm hitting a roadblock emotionally and the last thing I want to do is hurt him. We get along great, and I enjoy all the time we spend together."

They were both lost in thought, and the silence between the two of them stretched on for several minutes. Jackie finally pulled Liza in for a long hug.

"I don't know the answer, Cuz. But Cliff deserves the truth as soon as you can figure out just what that truth is."

"I know. I thought you could help me."

Jackie shook her head. "I'm at a loss. Sorry. It's something only you will be able to figure out. But don't tarry too long. Cliff's already in over his head, and I'm afraid he will never recover from another failed relationship. He took a leap of faith when he asked you out, hoping he found someone that he could spend the rest of his life with."

"Nothing like making me feel worse."

"Sorry, but it's the truth."

"Yes, it is. And that doesn't help me feel any better about the whole situation. One day I can see us getting married with children, and the next day I'm running away scared to death."

Soon after, Liza headed home with no answers to the multiple questions rolling around in her head. Jackie was right. She needed to figure her feelings out and try not to hurt Cliff in the meantime. If she was going to walk away, she'd better do it quickly.

The following Tuesday, all of the vice-presidents were

in a meeting with Mr. Jackson. Suddenly, Mrs. Carney came rushing through the door with a slip of paper. She murmured something to her boss, and he looked puzzled. They murmured to each other for a few moments, then she strode out. The team waited and wondered what had happened, since Mrs. Carney never interrupted meetings.

"Well, let's see. Where were we? Oh yes, being interrupted." He grinned and they all looked at each other. "I have a request from our branch in France to send someone over immediately to help with a project and teach them how it is supposed to be done. Evidently, the company has had a lot of turnover in staff lately and is having difficulty holding on to the right people." He turned and looked straight at Liza. "Ms. Augustine, it appears they are asking for you personally."

Liza's eyes popped wide open, and her mouth gaped. "What?"

"Yes. I guess someone named Pierre said you were to come, or no one comes. That's a little cheeky of him, I'd say."

She chuckled and pretty soon, was laughing so hard she almost fell out of her chair. The other people in the room wondered if she'd gone nuts, but Mr. Jackson waited patiently. Wiping the tears, she said, "Oh my, Pierre. He was here a year or so ago for a few months and we tried to recruit him, but he went back home. He must have gotten a promotion to be able to make that request."

"Well, are you going to go?"

"Do I have an option? I mean, you can request that I not leave, right?"

"I'll let you refuse if you want, but Mrs. Carney is checking into the background of what is going on over there and why the request was made in the first place.

You can let me know once I have more details."

"Okay. That will give me a little time to mull over the request and for you to see what I'd be walking into. It's a strange request since Pierre knows very well how to run projects."

"While Mrs. Carney is making some calls, I have a couple of contacts I can get ahold of, too." Liza nodded. "Do you have a passport?"

"I do, actually. I renewed it a couple of months ago."

"Well, they want you immediately, so that would have been a problem."

"I also haven't started my new project yet, so that could be handed off to someone else."

"Let's discuss the details after the meeting."

"Yes, sir."

The meeting was finally over, and Mr. Jackson and Liza went to his office to read over the details that Mrs. Carney dug up. He then called one of his peers in France and listened on speakerphone about how the division was in a critical situation. After hanging up, Liza thought it all sounded more than a little sketchy.

"I think Pierre's cry for help is more serious than we made it out to be. Do you think I can handle this situation, Mr. Jackson?"

"I do. I think you are the perfect person. You have a very analytical mind, and I believe, just like the day of your first presentation, that you can figure out what is happening around you very quickly. Whatever you need, just let me know."

"How long do you think I will need to be gone?"

"At least three months, maybe up to six, depending on how quickly you can get things shaped up over there. And since you know this Pierre guy personally, it will help to have someone on the inside. Otherwise, you are bucking the entire system."

Taking a deep breath she thought about Cliff. This was perfect timing to give her that break she wanted without hurting his feelings. "I'll leave Thursday on whatever flight I can get."

"Perfect. Now, let's figure out who the best person is to turn your projects over to, so we don't have to worry about that while you're gone."

Liza stopped by Carolyn's desk when she returned to her office. "I'm going to France for a few months to train the staff at our subsidiary."

She squealed with delight. "I wish I could go with you."

"I do, too. Anyway, I'll be gone anywhere from three to six months. It's an open-ended date. I leave on Thursday, so anything in my fridge and snack cupboard is yours. You can email me if you have any questions, but all of my workload will be transferred to other people for the time being."

"It sounds exciting."

"You know what? It is, isn't it? I'll take pictures and send them to you."

"You will? Wonderful. I can live vicariously through you, then."

"Mrs. Carney is making all of my arrangements since the division contacted her. I'm going to leave the office as soon as I finish up a few things. I need to go home and pack. Hmmm. I'm not sure what to wear for casual over there."

"Ooooh. Take as little as possible and buy French clothes. Then you will be really chic when you return."

Laughing, Liza agreed. "Now you're talking."

Liza left by four and rushed home to clean the apartment and do laundry. She sent a text to Jackie and asked if she could come over the next morning since she had taken the day off. By evening, the apartment was clean, so all she had to do was strip the bed and throw her towels in the washer before leaving for the airport on Thursday. Her flight wasn't until later in the morning, so she would have time to finish packing and fold the laundry. She wanted Wednesday to be family time. When she arrived at Jackie's, she and Aaron met her at the door. Liza was pulling a cooler behind her as she walked through the door and straight into the kitchen.

"What do you have there? And why did you take today off?"

"This stuff is from my refrigerator. I'm leaving for an assignment in France tomorrow."

"Oh, my gosh." She grinned, and then it diminished just as quickly. "Does Cliff know?"

"Not yet. We have our usual date at Charlie's tonight, though."

"He's not going to be happy."

"No, he's not."

"How long are you going to be gone?"

"That's the thing. I'm not sure. Maybe three months, or it could be twice that. They're having a lot of problems and need some help training and organizing. Pierre asked me to come. Or, I should say, demanded."

"Oh, Pierre. Yummy."

Liza shook her head. "Now you sound like Carolyn. Anyway, I brought an extra key to my apartment. Better late than never, I guess. I'll need you to pick up my mail once in a while. Or I can have it transferred back to your house."

"No, I'll pick it up. What about your bills?"

"Almost everything comes out automatically. The rent, utilities, and cable. If I get a bill for something, you can let me know and I'll pay it online. Just open the mail, and it will tell you whether it is automatically paid or not. But most of my statements come electronically anyway."

"Oh, Liza. I will miss you so much."

"I'll miss you, too. Maybe this is exactly what I need. Space and time for myself to figure things out."

"But Pierre…"

Interrupting, Liza frowned at her cousin. "Don't even go there. Pierre is just a friend and work acquaintance. Always has been, always will be. I promise. The more I think about it, the more I believe this is a good thing. I went from my trauma to your house, and then I got involved with Cliff. I need some me-time to sort out my feelings. No one to take care of me and I can be on my own."

"Are you sure?"

"No."

"At least you're being honest about feeling conflicted."

"Yeah, well, one thing I do know is that I'm here to spend time with Aaron while you empty my cooler." And that's exactly what she did.

Eventually, Liza said her goodbyes and left before they both bawled their heads off. Liza needed to run a few errands and then go home to pack a few more items. She was still trying to decide how much to take with her. She wondered if Carolyn might be right about not filling her suitcase. That way she would have room in her bag for anything she bought to bring home. But now it was time to meet Cliff. She wasn't looking forward to telling him about the trip. She texted him earlier to let him know she would meet him right after he got off work.

She was at Charlie's waiting for him when he walked in. The staff figured out right away they were meeting every Wednesday, and they always kept their table free, no matter how busy the café was or how late the couple arrived. Besides, they were great tippers. When Liza saw Cliff drive in, she ordered their usual meals. He gave her a quick kiss before sitting down.

"You left work early today, huh?"

"Nope. I took the day off."

"Wow. That never happens. Are you sick?"

"No. I just had stuff to do."

The waitress brought their meals, and they began eating. Liza talked about seeing Aaron and playing with him that morning, then regaled him with Aaron's antics. Cliff talked about a new job he landed. As they finished eating, Liza suggested they go for a walk. It was a beautiful evening, and she didn't want to break the news inside the café when she knew Cliff would become upset. They began their walk, and Cliff was trying to make plans for Saturday when Liza interrupted him.

"I have some news you won't be happy about." Glancing over and already seeing him frown, all she could do was hope for the best.

"Spill."

"I'm leaving tomorrow for France. I've been summoned to do some extensive training on how to set up projects and be successful."

Cliff stopped walking the minute she said France. "Pierre."

"Well, yes. He will be there, but that's not why I'm going."

Gritting his teeth, he growled, "Right."

He began walking again, but faster. He also let go of her hand. She took hold of his arm, tugged, and finally stopped him in his tracks. Here they were, out on the sidewalk, in full view of the public, and they were going to have their first fight.

"Cliff, Pierre is a workmate. He isn't any different than Carolyn, Mr. Jackson, or Casey. I mention names all the time. Why are you hung up on Pierre? We went over all this months ago."

He stiffened. "You two were awfully cozy when he was here."

"A friend, Cliff. A friend. We worked together, and he wanted to experience the BBQ. Are you saying you don't trust me? Is that what all this is about?"

Liza stared at Cliff while waiting for an answer, but he refused to address the question. She turned to walk back to her car while he remained silent. The ball was in his court now. She finally heard him walking behind her, and he eventually caught up. They walked side by side until she stood by her car. Neither one had said a word yet. Sighing, she unlocked her car and opened the door. As she moved to get inside, Cliff stopped her.

"Wait. I'm sorry. You asked if I trusted you. I do. But I don't trust Pierre."

"You waited a long time to tell me that. What don't you trust about him?"

"Nothing in particular, except he's French."

Liza scoffed at his answer. "You watch too much TV. I knew this wasn't going to go well."

He hesitated. "I love you, Liza. I want to marry you and have a family."

"I know, Cliff. I know. But we will have to wait to discuss this when I get back."

She gave him a quick kiss, then drove out of the parking lot, leaving him standing there in her dust.

13

Cliff watched Liza drive out of his life and toward Pierre's. Stomping to his car, he drove straight to Ray's place. He was furious by the time he got there, too. Liza already texted Jackie that the evening hadn't gone well. When Ray got home from work, Jackie filled him in on the latest developments and offered to help if needed. All he said was, "I got this." Ray sat on the front porch waiting for the inevitable visit. Right on cue, Cliff arrived, and Ray led him to the basement. If there was going to be yelling or cussing, he wanted Aaron to be as far away from it as possible.

Cliff paced frantically in front of Ray, who was sitting calmly at the bar. "She's leaving me for that stupid Frenchman. I can't believe I trusted her. Women. They're all the same. Here I wanted to get married and have kids. But no! She runs off to France to be with Pierre," he said in a shaky voice.

"Really? That's what she told you? Huh."

Cliff glanced at his best friend. "What do you know about it?"

"So, her exact words were that she was leaving you for Pierre?"

Cliff threw his cap across the room, and it bounced off the wall as he yelled. "No, she didn't say that. She didn't have to."

"I see. So, you're putting words in her mouth now." Cliff groaned and slumped onto one of the cushy chairs. "Start over. What exactly did she tell you?" He mumbled an answer, and Ray almost laughed at the situation. "What?"

He spat out, "She said something about they requested her to go over and do training or something. I don't know. Once she said France, I kind of zoned out."

"Who brought up Pierre?"

"I did."

"And?"

"Did Liza get all googly-eyed and swoon over his name like my wife does?"

"Oh, good grief. Of course not. She's not that type of woman."

"So, you got mad over someone she will be working with, and you don't even know him."

Cliff crossed his arms and pouted. "You don't either."

"Actually, I do. He came for supper more than once and we had a great time. I can see why Liza hit it off with him – as friends. He went back home to a woman named Felicia."

Cliff hung his head. "And I told her I trusted her, but she knew I didn't."

"So, what are you going to do about it?"

He shook his head. "I need to apologize right now before it's too late."

"Advisable."

Cliff grabbed his hat off the floor, tore up the steps two at a time, and shot out of the house. Ray eventually found Jackie in their bedroom.

"That was interesting."

"I heard him leave. Was he still mad? I couldn't tell."

"No. Totally embarrassed. The first thing he said was that Liza was leaving him for Pierre."

Jackie laughed. "I knew that was going to be a problem. Did you straighten him out?"

"He straightened himself out. All I had to do was

make him repeat what she really said. He had to admit that he was the one that brought up Pierre's name. He should be on his way to Liza's now."

"Should I warn her?"

"I don't know, what do you think?"

"I'll let it play out. They're adults."

Ray shook his head. "Maybe Liza is, but I'm not so sure about Cliff."

Liza shoved her suitcase by the door and wiped the tears from her eyes. Her car was parked inside the garage and locked up tight. She was already missing her apartment but was honored that she was requested to make the trip to France. Never having worked as a troubleshooter before, she decided that being a team leader on projects was pretty much that role, just on a smaller scale. Liza hadn't taken much time to study the information on the French division, but she would have plenty of time on the plane. Mrs. Carney emailed several more documents that she thought would be helpful.

Looking around the apartment, it looked like all she needed to do was get up, dress, and call for a ride-share. With the airline tickets available on her phone, all she needed to do was get something to eat later at the airport. Jackie was going to wash the bedding and towels, so Liza didn't even have to worry about that before leaving. She hoped for a good night's sleep, though. Wiping another tear, she realized that sleep was probably not on the agenda after all.

Suddenly, there was a pounding on her door. Liza ran to answer it due to the late hour. Shaking her head, she figured her neighbors probably thought that all of her visitors were the noisiest ones in town. She threw open the door, not knowing if the place was on fire or what.

Cliff barged in and turned to face her. Liza wasn't sure whether she wanted to close the door or not. They stared at each other for a moment before he grabbed her into a bear hug.

"I'm so sorry. So sorry. I don't want to lose you. I was so jealous. I'm so sorry."

Liza could hardly breathe, but she managed to flip the door shut before she gave Cliff her undivided attention. "What are you doing here?"

He finally released her and stared at her face. Taking in all of her features, he gave a brief smile, then leaned in to kiss her cheek. He didn't think she would accept one on the lips. "I had to come and apologize in person. I couldn't let you leave before I saw you again. I'm so sorry. I can't tell you that enough."

"Come over here and sit down. What changed your mind?"

"I needed to remember what you told me was your actual reason for leaving. I was so laser-focused on blaming Pierre, that I forgot it was your job."

"But you didn't trust me, Cliff."

"I know. Deep down I did, but I couldn't get there. Look, Liza. I'm sorry a million times over. I'll wait for you, as long as it takes."

Liza wasn't sure how to answer him, since she was so unsure of herself, let alone their relationship. "Cliff, we will keep in touch. But I need this trip. For me. I lost everyone I have ever loved, and I've come so far in the last year. I think this trip will be good for me overall. I can't commit to you yet. Something inside is too scared that I might lose someone else. Please allow me this time without making me feel guilty."

He held her hands and tears were pooling in his eyes.

"I'm such an emotional mess. I love you so much and don't want you to go. Being with you has been a big step for me, too. I'm ready for a commitment, but I forget that you had all that loss in your past." He sighed and swiped at his tears. "This is an amazing opportunity for you. How long did you say you'd be gone?"

"I don't know. Three to six months is what the company gauged. I need to train a bunch of inexperienced staff, plus educate the ones already there on how to do their jobs. This so-called opportunity might be completely over my head, but I won't know until I get there. Plus, the boss wants me to do a little snooping around. The place is a mess, and they want to know why. We may have to shut the division down if things don't work out. It scares me to death to walk into the unknown, and I just hope I can pull it off."

"That sounds pretty serious." He paused. "I can't believe I was so rude and didn't let you explain this the first time around." Sighing, he reached out and took both of her hands in his. "Can I stay the night?"

"No. You go home. I want to say my goodbyes tonight."

"Are you sure? I could take you to the airport tomorrow."

"I'm sure. It will be hard enough to get on the plane as it is."

Cliff stayed a little longer, but eventually, Liza pushed him out the door. Maybe she could get some sleep after all. Shutting out the lights, she slowly made her way to the bedroom.

14

Managing to get enough sleep, Liza felt rested when her alarm went off. Since she wasn't rushed, sleeping in would benefit her greatly with a long flight ahead of her. After Cliff came over and they worked out their differences, for the time being anyway, it was easier to settle in for the night.

Checking in at the airport, she had a leisurely breakfast and then found her gate. She called and let Jackie know what happened with Cliff the night before and reassured her that they would be fine. Secretly, she was hoping for the "distance to make the heart grow fonder" thing to happen. She also sent a text to Cliff. He was evidently waiting for her message, as she had an immediate response. Then she shut off her phone and boarded her plane. Mrs. Carney bought a first-class seat for her, and she didn't even realize it until she was checking in her bag. She decided she would have to pay her back dearly when she arrived home. Thank goodness, she could stretch out and do a little work at the same time.

Dozing a little seemed to make the trip go faster. But she was ready to be taken to her lodging to rest. Picking up her luggage, she found Pierre waiting for her. They hugged before he took her bags and found their way outside. Grabbing a taxi, they were swept away to an apartment building that was located close enough to the office that Liza could walk to work every day. She tried to take in the sights, but the time difference was killing her. Pierre insisted on a drink to celebrate her arrival, but he was going to have to wait.

The apartment was quaint and more comfortable than a hotel room. Pierre was sent on his way, much to his disappointment. He promised to stop in the morning and take her sightseeing. Needing to take those few hours of silence to work out the time change, food, and sleep were high on her agenda right then. The cupboards and small refrigerator were stocked with goodies, so that was a help. Liza soon emptied her suitcase and tucked it away. Then she proceeded to chuck her travel clothes, took a bath, and finally found something to satisfy her appetite. She hoped by Monday morning she would be acclimated to the time change, or she would be one grouchy woman.

As promised, Pierre arrived to take her around the city. His new wife, Felicia, joined them. She was gorgeous and accepted Liza as her friend. It probably helped when she found out about Cliff. Liza took selfies wherever she stopped. If the picture included the three of them, Liza made sure Felicia was standing between her and Pierre. Sending the pictures to Cliff, Jackie, and even Carolyn, she just wanted them to know she was safe and sound. She also let them know how much she loved meeting Felicia.

Begging off for more sightseeing on Sunday, Liza needed the day to relax and settle in. There was also the matter of the division going down the tubes in the last couple of years, and she knew what that meant. Either save it or recommend closing it down. For Pierre and Felicia's sake, she hoped that meant salvaging what was left.

Spending most of the afternoon scouring the information on the management team, she traced back to when things began to change from a profitable company to the complete mess they were in now. It was all too obvious when the changes began. By evening, her suspicions were all but confirmed. Since she hadn't stepped foot inside the building yet, she didn't want to enter the dragon's den with preconceived notions, but the paperwork showed a clear path of destruction. Why no one had done their due diligence up to now was beyond comprehension. Why did it take a call from Pierre to set things in motion? He didn't even have the power to make that call, but he did anyway.

By Monday noon, Liza had been introduced to multiple staff on the management team. The work structure was skewed with more bosses than regular staff. It was no wonder that production was in the tank. The money was going out the door with no one to produce the funding. Liza definitely had her hands full. The boss, Mr. Farthington, was from America. The two of them took an instant dislike of each other. He was personally running the place into the ground, and he certainly didn't want Liza to make any changes. He got the job when the previous vice-president had a heart attack and proceeded to retire. Mr. Farthington happened to be visiting the division, so he was installed in his place. The company evidently forgot about it being a temporary position and didn't check up on his ability to run the division in the first place. According to Liza's records, the board was becoming quite concerned and had been instructing Mr. Farthington to improve things quickly or they would replace him. Evidently, the man didn't believe it would happen since no action had happened on previous threats.

Now, it was time for drastic action. Liza wasn't going to pussyfoot around, or she would never be able to go home. They needed the big guns brought in right away.

She sent a lengthy email to Mr. Jackson to get his help. With the time changes, it would take a little patience to wait for an answer. But she was sure that by the end of the week, things would start to happen.

On Tuesday, Liza met with Pierre and his handpicked team. They met in a closed conference room and discussed their current project. She wanted all of the details, complaints, good ideas, bad ideas, and everything else in between, discussed at length. She also expected honest answers about their view of the company.

Mr. Farthington was unable to walk inside the room since the door was locked per Liza's instructions. He banged on the door and demanded to know what was going on. Liza opened the door slightly and politely refused his entry. "We are working on their assigned project, so please don't disturb us again." Liza shut the door in his face and locked it against the intruder. He fussed and fumed from the other side, but Pierre and Liza began where they left off. The show of strength against their boss helped the team form a bond, and they were finally able to get somewhere. Liza spent the day in the room teaching, training, educating, and bringing out the best in each person. Pierre kept them in food and water, along with translating where needed. Thankfully, there were bathroom facilities off to the side of the room and they didn't have to unlock the door. After they finished for the day, Pierre stated they had accomplished more in eight hours than they had in three weeks. In the past, Mr. Farthington had interrupted their meetings and kept changing their plans.

During a break in the meeting, Liza read an email from Mr. Jackson. He agreed to her advice and promised things would be happening soon. He had been working behind the scenes and found more interesting facts. He was glad to hear from Liza as soon as he did because he was ready to act anyway. By the following day and for the rest of the week, the division was beginning to swarm with suits from the lowest to the highest management positions. Chaos reigned, but a good kind of chaos. If the division was going to be saved, they needed a complete overhaul. How they got so many people in so quickly boggled her mind, but Mr. Jackson worked miracles. Even the board was involved.

Liza took Pierre's team and relegated them to a room out of the way. Then she took another team and spent the day with them, much as she had done the day before with Pierre's. This group was more rough-and-tumble and needed more training. They planned out the next week, and Liza made sure each person had a specific assignment to complete before each day began.

By the end of the week, Liza was exhausted. She had received several texts from Cliff and Jackie over the last few days, but Liza was too busy to reply to all of them. On Saturday, she sent lengthy texts to them both trying to explain what she had been doing and that she was going to spend the weekend lounging around her apartment trying to rest before tackling the mess the following week. She wasn't sure she had ever recovered from the time change, either.

Thinking back over the week, she felt like she could accomplish what she was assigned to do in three months. She would stay and get the current projects off the ground and see them through. She would also go between the two groups to problem-solve and help them learn their jobs well. Pierre's group caught on quickly, so Liza was sure most of her time would be spent overseeing the other team. Definitely needing a lot of polishing, they would be given all the tools they needed to be successful, she hoped.

Mr. Farthington was livid when the place began to swarm with additional overseers. He found himself under severe scrutiny, and the last straw was when the board members showed up and asked for a meeting. By the end of that impromptu get-together, Mr. Farthington was packing his bags. He was insolent to the board and everyone around him. Unexpectedly, many of the employees clapped as he was escorted out of the building. Their attitudes began to change immediately, and everyone was off to the races. A new boss would need to be in place soon, though. One which would be of Mr. Jackson and the board's choosing. Liza was afraid her boss would ask her to stay and take over, so she preemptively threatened Mr. Jackson in an email.

The next step was a reorganization of the job duties. Liza knew people's pride would be stepped on, along with a few toes. So many people were given titles for absolutely no reason. A few admitted to taking advantage of the weak leadership but wished to continue working for the company. Over the course of the next month, a few were insulted and walked out. The staff that stayed handled the reorganization pretty well. Keeping any job in the company was better than the unemployment line. Pierre would walk through occasionally and cheer everyone on. His great outlook was what made him popular with everyone, and it was welcome in the midst of the chaos. Pierre was happy with his job and didn't want an advancement. He loved managing projects and was proud of his work now that he was able to do so without interference.

As the weeks disappeared, and Liza's job was more or less routine, she began to enjoy her time in France. Pierre, Felicia, and Liza began traveling around the area and she tried out different foods. Felicia and Liza went shopping one day by themselves so Liza could buy some clothes. Of course, she needed trinkets to take back to Carolyn, too. Liza made sure she took a few pictures of the two of them shopping to send back to Cliff and Jackie.

Having friends to give personal tours was awesome. One evening, the three of them went out to a nice restaurant to celebrate. The couple announced they were going to have a baby, and Liza was thrilled for them. She shared a picture of Aaron more than once during her trip, and he was growing so fast. Pierre still talked about his experience with the BBQ and how much fun he had. One day, he hoped that they could come back to visit again as a family. Liza told him they would have another BBQ just for him.

Three months had come and gone, and the division was doing much better all the way around. The staff kicked in to save the place. The employees knew things were bad but hadn't realized how close they were to losing their jobs. The reorganization of management from top to bottom seemed to be working. Now the place was lean, mean, and working like a well-oiled machine.

Liza would soon be on her way home again. She hadn't given her relationship with Cliff much thought, either. Her workdays were exhausting, and she would spend most of the weekend resting or going over reports. Pierre and Felicia encouraged her to let them entertain her frequently. Being busy most of her free hours kept her mind constantly occupied with so many thoughts, but nothing led her to think of Cliff. His texts brought her back to earth, and she always had to think through her responses. She worried that she was going to break his heart when she returned home. Being away hadn't helped her make any decisions, one way or the other. Yes, she loved Cliff, but did she love him enough? Had she missed him these last few months? Not really, but she was also constantly busy with work. Even Jackie received very little contact from her. If she thought too long on the subject, she was rather ashamed of herself for dismissing her closest friends and family. But it was easier to not think about it at all.

Liza's flight home would land in the late evening, so she didn't tell Cliff or Jackie the exact time of her arrival. She wanted to be able to settle back into her apartment without them all over her. The time change was always a killer, anyway. She also wanted to drop off a few things at the office before going home. Liza had several reports and a few trinkets for Carolyn and wanted them available for the girl when she reported for work the next day. Liza didn't plan to be in the office until the following week and didn't want to wait to hand in the reports. Sometimes the best-laid plans don't always pan out.

15

Flying the great blue skies, Liza stretched out and thought about going home to Cliff. What would she say to him when they saw each other? She missed him, loved him, and cared for him. But she didn't know if she wanted to marry and have children. A part of her said, "Absolutely yes", yet the scared part said, "No way." She thought about her marriage to Jason, but it didn't last long enough to have many memories. If she hadn't miscarried and she had been raising a child, what would be her feelings now? Her child would be seven years old. All those years gone by, and she still hesitated about getting married again. Liza wasn't sure why things weren't clearer for her after being gone for all those weeks. She could solve a multitude of corporate issues, but not a simple thing like marrying a man she loved. She got nowhere, and the closer she got to arriving home, the more she worried about making the wrong decision.

Landing, getting her luggage, and then calling for a ride was all done with her foggy brain. She felt bone-tired. More tired than she thought she would be. Liza was soon whisked away to her office building. The driver promised to stay put and then take her home to her apartment. Her work valise was full of papers that she needed to drop off, so she left everything else in the car, including her phone and purse. She said she would be gone ten or fifteen minutes, tops. All she needed to do was take the elevators to her office, and with no one there that time of night, she wouldn't have to talk to anyone. Anxious to get back to the car and home, Liza rushed over to the elevators, saying hello to the night shift that was lounging behind the desk.

The driver sat singing to a song on the radio as she hurried through the front doors. As a safety feature, any after-hours staff had to code in or use a badge to access the elevators, or any of the ground-floor doors to the stairs. Liza was soon zipping up to her floor. She filled Carolyn's inbox with several files, then placed a couple of gifts, strategically located right smack dab in the center of her desk so she would see them first thing in the morning. Liza wished she could be there to see the look on Carolyn's face.

She checked her office and noted the musty smell. Evidently, no one had been in there for a long time, so she left the door wide open. Carolyn would chuckle, knowing what that meant. She made a mental note to refill her snack cupboard and refrigerator when she returned on Monday. Tomorrow, she would need to go grocery shopping anyway. Turning from her office door, she began making her way to the elevators. All of a sudden, the back of her neck tingled, and as she started to turn, a hand grabbed her neck from behind and another slapped over her mouth. The scream was muffled, and her valise went flying.

"Shut up," someone whispered in Liza's ear.

She tried to bite her attacker, but his grip was pushing so hard against her mouth and neck that she couldn't bite, scream, or jerk away. Her heart rate felt like it was beating a million miles an hour, and with little oxygen, she worried about fainting.

"Come on," the man said.

He pulled her backwards to the stairwell and then pushed her to the floor, cracking her head on the wall as she landed. Blacking out for a moment, she lost any hope of getting help. All she could see were stars when she tried opening her eyes. Suddenly, a blindfold was placed, a gag stuffed in her mouth, and while she was still struggling from hitting her head, her hands were tied behind her back. It all happened so quickly; she couldn't believe it.

"Get up." With the man pulling and yanking on her bindings, she managed to get to her feet, swaying as she stood up. "Go down the stairs." Dizzy, all she could envision was flying down cement steps and not living through the fall.

The man guided her to the edge of the first step, and Liza felt with her toes for each step. Slow and tedious on her part, whoever this guy was, he was impatient with her. She began counting ten steps, a landing, ten steps, a landing, and on and on until he pushed her through a door. The smell was different, and it certainly was not office space. The sounds were more like a mechanical room. He pushed and pulled until she was eventually jammed into what she assumed was a closet. Small and stuffy, at least he wasn't torturing her.

After a few minutes of quiet, her mind began to clear. Liza then wondered what happened to her driver. He had all her luggage, purse, and phone. She figured this guy didn't want her purse because he never asked for any money, but he must have wanted her. No, she thought. How would the guy know she was going to be there? Now what? Fear took hold of her again, and she began to shake. She had to think. How was she going to get out? Liza didn't hear a sound from the man, which frightened her more. She was exhausted from her trip, stuck in what she assumed was a closet, blindfolded, hands tied behind her back, and a gag in her mouth. What a mess she was in.

*****

Looking at the clock, the driver waited fifteen minutes, then twenty. He was missing out on other rides and wondered where she was. All of her things, including her purse, were still in the backseat. He shook his head and figured she was either really trusting or very tired. He tried to call her, but her phone was in the car, too. Finally, after thirty minutes, he went inside and enquired about his ride. She never came back down the elevators, and the light was still lit up for her floor. He wasn't allowed near the elevators, but the security guard offered to go up and check around. Even he was beginning to be concerned when he found out the driver had all of Liza's belongings. He took a different elevator up so the driver could watch for the other one to come back down.

The guard found Liza's valise on the floor, and her office door was wide open. No one was around and everything was quiet. That's what frightened him the most. The quiet. Where could she be? He opened the elevator doors, but she wasn't there. Then he looked down the stairwell but didn't see or hear anyone. That's all the farther he was going on his own. He called the police and said he would meet them in the lobby.

The driver was still waiting to find out what to do when the guard's elevator returned. Now they had to wait for the police. At first, the driver was mad at losing all his wages for the night but realized that this had probably turned into a very serious situation. He completed the ride on his phone and the woman's card was charged a large amount for the time. He was satisfied that all was not lost, but he also felt a little guilty, too.

The police arrived, and the driver told his story. Then

the guard took the officers upstairs to her office space. The only way down was the elevator or stairs, and since the elevator was still on her floor, they began the long trek down the stairs. Arriving at the main floor with Liza nowhere to be found, one officer continued down and the other called for the fingerprint team.

The place was filling up with officers by the time people arrived for work. Carolyn was thrilled to find her gifts, and the pile of files would be gone through later that day. Then she was told that Ms. Augustine was missing, and an officer scolded her for touching her gifts before he could get fingerprints. She glared at him and told him that Ms. Augustine brought the gifts to her from France and to get over himself. She refused to let him touch them. Carolyn guarded her desk like a warden and tucked her gifts in her handbag, out of reach. Although she finally let them dust for prints on her desk, she kept her purse with her and out of reach at all times. Of course, she had to be fingerprinted, too.

Eventually, she was able to answer the phones and do her other work, including working on the files that Ms. Augustine dropped off. By the end of the day, the activity quieted around the office, and Carolyn finally broke down and cried. Mrs. Carney happened to stop by on her way home, gathered Carolyn in her arms, and then walked her to the elevators. They were both in a bit of a shock.

The police called Jackie mid-morning and let her know Liza was missing. Someone would keep her informed as the case developed, and she was to let them know if her cousin showed up at her home. Jackie fell apart and called Ray. He rushed home to check on her, then drove over to the office building. No one could or would tell him anything, so he returned home and took care of Aaron. Now he would have to call Cliff before the poor guy heard about it on the news. The cameramen and reporters were all over the outside of the office building, and he was sure it was probably on the radio, too. Cliff was going to be as devastated as he and Jackie were.

Ray finally decided to tell him in person. He felt that was a better choice than on the phone. Jackie told him that she and Aaron would be fine. Struggling with how to tell Cliff, Ray was happy he was in a meeting for a few more minutes to give him the strength to pull this conversation off.

Cliff saw Ray in the waiting room and frowned. "What's the matter? Are Jackie and Aaron okay?"

"Yeah, fine. Can we talk in private?"

"Sure." They went into his office and closed the door. "Spit it out, man. You're scaring me."

"Liza is missing."

"Say what? You mean she didn't make the plane?"

"No. She made it to town, stopped off at her office, and disappeared."

"That makes no sense."

"I know. All the police can tell us is that the driver promised to wait outside while she dropped off a few things. They know she went up to her floor in the elevator, but it never came back down. After waiting for a half-hour, the driver came inside and asked about her. They all got worried enough that a guard went to her floor to see what the problem was. No one could find her. There was an empty work bag on the floor, her office door was open, and that's it."

"How can that be?"

"That's what everyone else wants to know. The cameras show her going up, but there isn't a trace of her after that."

Cliff dropped into his chair with a thud. "I don't understand."

"None of us do." Ray sat down across from him. "I'm sorry. I'm feeling just as helpless as you are. But I wanted you to know before you heard it from someone else or on the news."

"I appreciate that. What can I do?"

"Let the police know if you hear from her. That's all they asked us to do."

They both sat looking at the floor, lost in thought. Ray finally got up. "I better get back home. I've got my hands full between Jackie and Aaron. Stop by anytime, though."

"Okay. Thanks for stopping and telling me in person. This situation just doesn't make any sense."

"No, it doesn't." Ray let himself out and solemnly drove back home.

Cliff was worthless the rest of the day, so he left and went straight to Ray's. There was so much to look forward to with Liza coming home. How could one person disappear in thin air like that? He, Ray, and Jackie asked themselves that and many other questions over and over again. With no obvious answers available to them, no one felt any better by the time midnight rolled around.

Aaron was cranky all day and evening, and Jackie blamed herself. Sensing Momma was upset, so was he. Ray carried him to the bedroom, and they played before reading a book and settling his boy in for the night.

For three days, there was no word. Jackie feared the worst, and even if Ray was reassuring, he began to lose hope, too. Cliff's behavior at work was so pathetic, that they gave him a week of vacation and shoved him out the door. He sat at home and stared at the walls.

16

Liza woke up confused, sore, cramped, and needing to use the bathroom. She had no idea what time it was because of the darkness. She also forgot she had a blindfold on. At some point in time, while she was sleeping, the gag fell out of her mouth. When she tried to yell, her throat was so dry she could hardly swallow, let alone make any sounds. Remembering she was sitting in what was presumably a closet, she worked her way into a standing position and proceeded to crack her head on a low-hanging shelf. And to top it off, it was the same spot she had hit on the wall when she had been kidnapped. It hurt like the devil, and she just about knocked herself out again.

Using her bound arms behind her, she felt around to see if she could locate the doorknob. It took quite a bit of maneuvering in the small space, but eventually, she felt it, and then realized it was locked. She began to kick the door and make enough noise to alert someone to her presence. Someone finally did hear. Her captor. She could hear him say something, so she waited. Finally, Liza could hear not only one lock but two being released. The definitive sound of the door opening was a relief.

"Quit making a racket."

"I need to use the bathroom," she croaked out.

He grabbed her numb arms and pulled her along. "Come on."

"I can't see, and I won't be able to do anything with my hands tied."

"I'll untie your hands until you're done. Turn around."

Her arms dropped free but were tingling and painful to move. Even her shoulders felt like they had been pulled out of their sockets because they had been tied for way too long. She wasn't sure she could use her arms, so Liza shook them to try and restore some circulation. "Leave your blindfold on. I'll be watching you. It's right in front of you."

"I can't go to the bathroom if you're watching."

The man grumbled something under his breath. "Go now or forget it."

Liza stumbled into the bathroom and felt her way around. The walls felt dirty, but what choice did she have? She figured it was probably a good thing she couldn't see. When she finished, she asked, "Is there a sink so I can wash my hands and get a drink?"

"To your left."

No sooner had she taken a cooling drink than she was rushed back to the closet. He tied her arms again, and that dirty rag was stuffed back into her mouth. She heard the door locks click into place, then it was quiet again. She sat down on the floor and cried. She was hungry, and her belly growled and complained about only being offered a little water when it needed so much more. She rested her head against the wall and wondered how long she would be held and why. She didn't know why she didn't ask or attack him when her hands were free, but she wasn't strong enough to fight off a man, anyway. She had no idea where she was either, so where would she run to if she did get free? Liza had an analytical mind, so she figured she better use it instead of sitting there feeling sorry for herself.

With nothing better to do, Liza sat for hours thinking. She managed to spit the gag out of her mouth soon after the door was locked. She never heard anyone outside the door, so why bother yelling? She needed to save her energy for when she could alert someone to her presence.

Going down a mental list, she had so many questions, but no answers. What happened to her driver and all of her belongings? Who would her captor be? Was it the driver that did this? Of course not. He couldn't get upstairs. Who would it be instead? How would he know she was going to be there? He couldn't. She was a convenient target. So, he took whomever they ran across. What was he doing there in the first place? Robbing or stealing protected information on their projects? How did he get to that floor without being detected? By elimination, it had to be someone who worked for the company and knew their way around. Now she needed to start eliminating suspects.

All women were out. This was definitely a man. Okay, she thought. Size. Calculating from when he led her down the steps, he wasn't much taller, but broader. His voice was deep, and it quavered a bit, along with a shakiness in his hands. Who worked there that fit that description? Maybe someone who was not very sure of himself. She supposed he was afraid of getting caught. Mr. Jackson was over six feet tall and built like a football player. That also wasn't his voice. This guy wasn't that big, and he had some kind of odor about him. Something unusual Liza couldn't place. He also hadn't showered lately. What was that smell? She would have to come back to that and pay more attention the next time he opened the door.

So, where did she end up? Thinking about all the steps they went down, Liza knew they had gone down several flights. She was so concerned about keeping her feet under her that she didn't think about counting the floors as they went. There was another locked door that the man opened. She could hear the clearance of the lock. Yes. Someone who worked there had nabbed her. Liza felt like she was getting somewhere now. She shook her head and continued.

The man opened the door, and she remembered the rumbling of the air conditioning units. Definitely the mechanical room. So, they had walked all the way down to the basement. Too bad she didn't get any of that fresh air piped into her stale-smelling closet. The basement would be seldom visited, except for routine maintenance or problem-solving. Then a thought hit her. Maybe one of the maintenance men took her. Could that be who it was? Sure. They would have access to every part of the building. But why in the semi-darkness of her office? Liza kicked herself for not flipping on the lights upon her arrival. There were always a few soft lights shining so you could get around, and she didn't even think about it at the time. Was he hiding in her office or out in the main area? She didn't know how he sneaked up on her or where he came from. The questions continued to come back full circle. She had a reason for being there, but this guy didn't. What was his reason to be sneaking around?

Her thoughts were interrupted by the locks jiggling. The door opened and something dropped on her lap. She could smell French fries. Then the door shut. Liza yelled out. "Hey! I can't eat with my hands tied behind me." The door reopened and her bindings were roughly removed. The door slammed shut again, but she didn't care. Her hands were free. She tore off the blindfold and blinked several times. Nope, it was still pitch black. She grabbed the sack and devoured the fries. They were still warm and tasted delicious. There wasn't anything else in the bag except a napkin, but she was grateful anyway. Now, she was thirsty from the salty fries, but at least her gut was happier. She wadded up the bag and tossed it down by her feet.

Laying her head back again, the thoughts about what she could do to protect herself or have an advantage the next time the captor opened the door eluded her. Liza was now free to move within her small confines, which helped her achy muscles. She stood up and felt around on the shelf above her to see if there was something she could use as a weapon. All she found was a small roll of trash bags and some paper towels. Nothing of any assistance at all. If there was a shelf above that, Liza couldn't tell because she couldn't feel anything but empty space. She even felt for a light switch or a pullstring so she wouldn't be in the dark. Nothing. An old mop bucket was at her feet, but no mop handle. She felt a can or two sitting in the corner but dismissed them when she felt the rust crumble on her fingers as she touched them. Something sticky was on the floor by one of the cans. Grossed out, she wiped her fingers on her pants. She considered asking him to remove the bucket so she could stretch out more but figured he wasn't too concerned about her comfort.

Sighing, she sat back down. She needed to stay limber, so she exercised her arms and legs the best she could. More than once she cracked an elbow on the wall or door jamb, but her body felt better with the movement. Being tied up for so long had certainly affected her health. She was tired already. Liza blamed it on jet lag, the stress of being captured, and the lack of sustenance. Maybe if she faked being dead, he would leave her alone. Laughing, she figured all he would have to do was pinch her and she would complain. She decided to go back to being analytical but was asleep before she came up with her first question.

For what she calculated was three days, Liza was taken to the bathroom once a day and given some small token to eat. The only water she got was at the sink after she washed her hands. She was in a weakened state, and her captor didn't even tie her hands or use the blindfold. He always stayed behind her, so she never saw him. All she knew was that it was definitely the mechanical room, and her cage was a small closet. Knowing no one would find her unless someone came to the basement to check on the equipment, Liza was disheartened and was giving up. She asked the question, "Why?" but never received an answer. She was no closer to the truth than the day she was taken. Her mind began to play funny games on her, and she began to have conversations with imaginary people. When she reached out, no one was there. In her more lucid moments, she knew she didn't have much more time left. She was dehydrated and starving. Death seemed to be coming awfully fast for her, and she didn't know why.

17

Cliff sat with Ray in the den. He had been coming over every day to see if Jackie heard anything new. News crew vans were hanging out in front of the house as soon as they heard of the relationship between Jackie and Liza. Any visitors used the back door to come and go to escape the mob. There was protection from prying eyes by a gated fence in the back, and Ray was staying home from work to protect his family. He ran errands, and while out, he would stop by the police station to check to see if there was any new information. No way did he want Jackie to have to deal with the vultures parked outside. At least they stayed by the curbside. On day four, a policeman came to the house. Ray led him into the kitchen where Jackie was feeding Aaron, and Cliff was finishing his sandwich.

"Jackie, this is Inspector Parnelli. He wanted to update us on the case."

"Inspector. Please sit. Can I make you a sandwich or would you like a cup of coffee or something?"

"Nothing right now. I appreciate you asking, though. I'll be brief. We don't have anything else to report, and I just wanted to touch base with you."

Cliff was fuming. "I don't understand. How can she just disappear like that?"

Inspector Parnelli looked over at Cliff. "And you are?"

"Cliff McFarland."

Ray jumped in. "Ray's been my best friend for over twenty years and is part of my family. When Liza came up missing, I went to tell Cliff right away."

"I see. Where were you the night she disappeared?"

Cliff's mouth dropped open. "What?"

"Do you have an alibi?"

Everyone around the table gasped. Ray was able to speak first. "Are you kidding me?"

The inspector continued to look directly at Cliff. "Well," Cliff gulped. "No, sir. I live by myself."

"Hmmm. And what is your relationship with Ms. Augustine?"

"She's my fiancée. Liza's been in France for work, for the past three months or so, and we were waiting for her to finish her assignment to plan our wedding. She told me she would call when she arrived home. I never received a call. Now I know why."

"Don't leave town. We may have more questions."

"I'm not going anywhere. You need to find Liza."

The inspector ignored Cliff. "Ma'am. Please call if you hear anything." He laid his card on the table, then left the house.

Jackie said little until the inspector was gone. "How dare he accuse Cliff."

Ray went over to Aaron and cleaned up the lunch mess. "He didn't outright accuse him, sweetheart."

Cliff grumbled. "He might as well have. They always blame the husband or boyfriend in these cases. I should have kept my mouth shut."

Ray picked up Aaron and tickled his tummy. They both giggled. "That's my boy." Ray looked back at Jackie and Cliff. "Look. Everyone is suspect. They feel like fools because they can't figure it out. I have another idea if you're willing to listen." They both nodded. "I've been mulling this over for a couple of days, and now that the inspector was here, I think we need a new plan."

Cliff agreed. "Go ahead. I'm up for anything right now."

"How about we hire a private investigator?" Jackie and Cliff looked at each other. "I mean, the police are stumped, so they are missing some big clue. No one has contacted us about a ransom, and if she was at the office and disappeared without even going back down the elevators, then where is she?"

Jackie took Aaron. "I'll go change his diaper. I can't even talk about this anymore."

The men watched her leave the room, then Cliff said, "Do you know one?"

"No. But when all this went down, a friend of mine mentioned he knew someone who ran an agency. What do you think?"

"We need someone to find her, so I'm game. I don't think we have anything to lose here. The cops certainly can't find her, and I don't like being a suspect."

"Okay. I'll see if I can get a number to call."

Ten minutes later, Ray hung up the phone and was waiting for a private investigator to show up. He instructed him to use the back door and stood outside watching for him to arrive. Twenty minutes later, Ray led him inside.

"Alex Mayfair at your service. Like I mentioned on the phone, I've heard the media version. Let's hear your side."

Ray explained about the police calling Jackie when Liza disappeared without a trace. And since there had been no leads, they were frantic to find her. When the investigator stopped by the house and made Cliff feel guilty, that's when Ray knew they had to do something. He went over all that they were told about her disappearance, and how they just couldn't believe that someone could just disappear without a trace inside the corporate office like that.

"That's all we know. Liza disappears, but no explanation as to how. I mean, did they check the ductwork, the ceiling tiles, or the elevator shaft? How can she go up the elevator and then disappear? Someone has missed a step somewhere."

"It sounds like it." Alex watched Cliff pacing and mumbling to himself. "What's up with him?"

"Investigator Parnelli asked him if he had an alibi. He's been freaking out ever since."

"I see."

"Liza is his fiancée. Well, maybe not technically, but she will be. They were going to discuss it when she got back from France."

Alex nodded. "That's why he's a suspect."

"I suppose so."

"I better get to work then. Is there someone at the company who can get me inside access? I need to work without interference from the cops."

"Cliff, come over here and quit your pity party for a moment."

He stopped his pacing and came closer. "What? Can't a guy worry about being thrown in jail?"

"Alex needs people inside Liza's company. Give him some names that he can trust to help him."

"Oh. That's easy. Carolyn is her secretary. They get along really well. Mr. Jackson is the boss. Let's see. One of the newer VPs is named, uh, Casey, I believe. Liza really likes her."

"Just the people I need. I'll start with Carolyn."

"When can you start?"

"Right now. I've cleared my schedule. This is a lot more important than anything I have on the books. Does she have any enemies that you know of?"

"Heavens no. She's liked by everyone."

"An abduction is usually planned, but no one knew what time she would be home, right?"

Cliff nodded. "Right. She was going to call when she got home, but if it was late, then the plan was to call us when she got up the next day. You know, jet lag and all. That's why none of us worried about not hearing from her that night."

"Okay. I've got a little background work to do before I go to her office. Tomorrow, I will visit Carolyn. I need which floor Liza's office is on."

Ray and Cliff looked at each other and shrugged. Ray went to find Jackie to ask her. Cliff said, "I've never been to her office. She's a vice-president, and I get a little squeamish around people with fancy titles."

Ray returned. "The twentieth floor. The secretary handles five offices, so Jackie says she should be able to help you with anything you need."

"Good."

After Alex left, so did Cliff. He wanted to worry and pace without interruption. When he pulled up to his house, he didn't realize he had company. A policeman walked up to him as he opened the door.

"Mind if I come in?"

Cliff froze in place. "Why?"

"Do you mind if I search your house?"

"Yes, just on the principle of the thing. Do you have a search warrant?"

"I will have shortly."

"Fine. When it arrives, come on in. I'll leave the door

unlocked. But until then, stay put."

The policeman nodded and took a seat on the porch. Cliff went inside and called his lawyer, who agreed to come right over. The warrant and his lawyer arrived around the same time as each other. Cliff sat in his recliner with the warrant in hand and watched the police start looking through the house. The lawyer rushed inside and looked at the warrant. Then he followed the men at a respectable distance. Just enough that he wasn't in their way, but close enough to observe. Two hours later, the police left empty-handed, with not even an odd fingerprint to be found.

Cliff scratched his chin. "We didn't have time to discuss this before I asked you to come running over, but what would be they looking for?"

"I don't think they know. They were trying to find something of Liza's I would guess. Or a weapon."

"I don't think Liza's been here more than a time or two, and that was only a brief visit. I think I was picking something up and she never even sat down. But I'm not off the hook yet, right?"

"No, probably not. Someone will be tracking you."

"Thanks for coming over."

"You did the right thing by calling me. Your place didn't get trashed, and they know you have retained a lawyer. You sat in your chair like a good boy and behaved, too. I'm just a phone call away if you need me for anything else."

"Good to know."

The lawyer laughed. "No need for them to know I'm a divorce lawyer." Even Cliff laughed at that and walked him to the door.

Cliff still had a few days of vacation left, so he planned to continue his routine of driving over to Ray's for a couple of hours. He would either go to the grocery store or get takeout. Otherwise, he planned to stay at home and be the most boring person they ever had the pleasure of watching.

18

Alex Mayfield thought of himself as a nice guy, but if needed, he could hold his own with the bad guys. As a private investigator, he learned to be self-sufficient, and more than once he solved a crime the police couldn't. Naturally, they weren't happy when he arrived on the scene. He pushed the elevator button and waited. One of the senior police officers came over and stood beside him.

"What are you doing here?"

"Visiting a friend."

"You have no friends."

Alex laughed, the doors opened, and he got on the elevator. As the doors were closing, he wiggled his fingers in a wave at the officer. Before long, he was standing in front of Carolyn's desk and introduced himself.

"Ma'am, I'm Alex Mayfield." He flipped open his badge. "I'm a private investigator and have been hired by Ms. Augustine's family to find her. Would you be able to help me get the information I need?"

"Mr. Mayfield, I'd be delighted to help you. No one else seems to be able to find her. What can I do to help?"

"Show me around your floor. Talk about Ms. Augustine's daily routine for me."

"You bet. Let me transfer my phone to someone else so we can talk uninterrupted."

"Perfect."

Carolyn explained Liza's normal routine. "She would come off the elevator, pass my desk, then go into her office. When I came back to work that morning, I found her files in my tray, and she left some gifts for me in the middle of my desk. I opened them before I realized she was missing."

"So, she would have gone into her office every morning first thing."

"Yes, sir. And I know she was in there because the door was open."

"Open? Why is that significant?"

"Because Ms. Augustine always has her door open. She only closes it at night when she goes home or needs to make some calls. The door was closed the whole time she was gone to France, and it was closed when I went home that night. But when I came in the next morning, it was open, so I knew it was her that dropped off the files and gifts, and not just a courier."

"Okay. We've established she was actually here, then. Show me any other exits."

"Just the stairwell. No one uses them unless we have a fire drill. We're so high up and all."

"Show me where the door is located."

"Sure. This way."

"And the cops checked it all out?"

"That's my understanding. They swarmed the place for several hours. When I arrived, a few had been through the office already and completed the first walk-through. That was my understanding. Then all of a sudden, the place was flooded with cops everywhere."

"Do you have access to the stairs from the main floor?"

"After five in the evening, the only way to use the elevator or open the door to the stairs is by keycard, or you have to punch in your code. When you're terminated, then those are deactivated. Each person has their own numbers."

"All individually assigned."

"Correct. That way it is trackable."

"You've been very helpful. Is Mr. Jackson around?"

"I don't know. I can call his secretary and find out."

"I should probably be in touch with him before I begin traipsing around the building."

"Just a moment." Carolyn picked up her phone and hit a button. "Mrs. Carney, this is Carolyn. I have a private investigator here who would like to see Mr. Jackson. He was hired by Ms. Augustine's family. Yes. Okay. Thank you." She hung up the phone and turned to Alex. "She said to go on up. One more floor and to your right."

"Thank you. You've been tremendously helpful. I hope to see you again, soon."

"Just find her, Mr. Mayfield."

"I'll do my best. And you can call me Alex." He smiled and headed to the elevator.

Alex spent the next hour or so visiting Mr. Jackson and gleaned as much information as he could. He needed background information on Liza, what the police had done, and what they were doing now. Was there anyone at the company that resented her? With the hour getting late in the day, all he had gotten done was walking around and figuring out the layout of the building. Mr. Jackson called the security office and asked for the name of the man who called the police that night, but he wouldn't arrive back to work until the following afternoon. Alex had plenty to do before he talked to the man. This was already day five and time was ticking away.

Before leaving for the day, he walked down the stairs from Liza's floor until he got to the bottom. The door was locked, and the sign stated it was a mechanical room. He went back up a flight and came out on the main floor. Glancing at his watch, he didn't have time to get anything else done today, but he had a list of people to talk to starting first thing in the morning. He also had Mr. Jackson's blessing to follow every lead, and to call him or Mrs. Carney if there was a problem getting access to anyone or anything he needed.

*****

Liza was in bad shape. Not being able to move around in her cramped position, she hurt all over. And there was always a terrible odor that she couldn't place. She didn't smell good, either, from days without washing. Somewhere along the way, she had soiled her pants. Not having eaten or drank anything for what seemed like days, her captor hadn't opened her door for a long time. She didn't know if it was hours or days. Liza lost track of time and wasn't lucid enough to keep track. She guessed ignoring her was his way of killing her slowly, and it was working.

When she was thinking clearly, she fretted over Jackie, Ray, and Cliff. Aaron was too small to miss her. Liza loved Cliff, and he was waiting for her. Her fear of commitment went away at the moment of abduction. Jackie was right, as usual. You never know how much time a person has, so why did she waste her time by denying her relationship with Cliff? Now, she couldn't even cry anymore. Her body was too dry, and all she could do was pray someone would find her in time.

*****

Day six arrived, and Alex felt antsy. He rushed back to the office building and located the IT department. He explained who he was and why he was there. Then he mentioned Mr. Jackson's name if they needed to check on him. They did.

"Okay. We have the go-ahead. What can we help you with?"

"I understand the keycard access is denied once a person has left their employment. Correct?"

"Yes. As soon as we are notified, we deny all access to computers, doors, and elevators. Anything that the card could access is wiped clean."

"So, what happens if someone gets missed?"

"Then they would still have access, of course."

"Can you tell me how many employees are no longer working here, in the last six months?"

"No, we don't keep any record like that. You'd have to talk to the Human Resource department."

"Can you generate a list of employees that no longer have access? I find that hard to believe you wouldn't be able to do that."

"Oh, well. I suppose, but it will take a little bit to figure out how to run that report."

"I'll wait. Then I will head over to the Human Resource department like you suggested."

The IT director eventually brought a huge list of names to Alex but hesitated to give him the paperwork. "You can check with Mr. Jackson again if you wish. I promise I won't be taking this paper out of the building." They handed the pile over grudgingly.

Looking down at his watch, it had taken over an hour for them to run the report and get it printed off. He rushed toward the HR department next and asked to see the director. He went through his whole spiel again, and they contacted Mr. Jackson's office once again. At least the staff was consistently careful about releasing information to a stranger. He liked that. Alex explained what he needed and why. The HR director printed out her list of discharged employees and began working down each name, comparing the two lists. Thankfully, they were both alphabetical in nature, so it was faster than digging through sheets to match up names. Twenty minutes later, the director stopped for a moment, circled one in red, and then continued. By the time she was done, she went back to the name she circled.

"I have one name here that I've completed the paperwork on, but IT doesn't have him listed."

"And that name is?"

"Nathan Lantry. Let me see. A few months ago, he went off his rocker and was institutionalized. That's the rumor anyway."

"Was the IT department not notified or did someone drop the ball on their part?"

"I'll check." The woman pulled a file and dug through all the paperwork. "My file is complete, but that doesn't mean it didn't slip through the crack somewhere between here and there. We usually send a paper memo plus an email." She scanned her email and finally found her request. Printing it out, she handed it over to Alex.

"Thank you. You have been most helpful. And please don't mention anything about this situation while I'm working on the case."

"No problem. My lips are sealed. And good luck."

"Thank you. Have a nice day."

Here he was looking at his watch again. The day was running away from him, and Alex had so much to do, still. The morning was gone, so he headed to the cafeteria, bought lunch, and sat down to think about what had happened those first few days after Liza disappeared. A piece of the puzzle was missing. What was it? Why couldn't they find Liza? She hadn't been missing that long before the search started. It had to be that someone didn't do their job.

Alex handled a few calls and emails before riding the elevator back up to the top floor. He walked down the whole staircase once again until he arrived at the mechanical room. Puzzled, he made his way to the security office and waited for the gentleman he needed to return to work.

"Mr. Mayfield, I'm Gary Cooper. And before you say anything, yes, my mother was crazy about the actor."

Alex smiled. "You get that a lot, I presume."

"All my life, but not as much as I used to. This younger generation has no idea who he was. Now. What can I do for you?"

"Would you tell me how things went down when Ms. Augustine disappeared?"

"Sure."

Gary explained how the driver waited twice as long as Ms. Augustine mentioned she would be gone and was very irritated because she hadn't returned yet. He was losing jobs just sitting out there waiting for her.

"I wasn't off duty yet and happened to be by the front desk when she arrived, and then again when the driver came in to find her. So, I offered to go to the office and find out if she was okay or still needed a few minutes. The elevator she took was still on her floor, so I took a different one. Just a gut feeling I had that something wasn't right. I found her empty bag on the floor, her office door open, and she was nowhere to be found. I called out her name several times as I did a quick check of all the other offices and rooms. Then I looked down the stairwell, but I didn't see or hear anything. I even checked inside the elevator she rode up. That's when I called the police."

Alex nodded. Everyone's stories were much the same thing. "So did you follow along with the police or were they on their own?"

"I went with them everywhere, including walking down the stairs. I gotta tell you, I was glad we weren't going up. When we arrived on the main floor landing, one of the officers continued down the last flight to look around and the other one entered the lobby area."

"How long was it before the second officer returned?"

"Just a couple of minutes."

"What did he say to the other officer?"

"All clear." Alex contemplated the situation and waited for Gary to come to the same conclusion. "But he couldn't get into the mechanical room because it's locked, right?"

"True. The officer couldn't clear a room he couldn't get into. And he just assumed that no one else could, either, instead of having you unlock the door. Would the same access to the doors on the stairwell work with the mechanical room?"

"Yes. Do you want me to unlock it for you?"

"Not yet. I have one more idea that just came to me. Let's head to the IT department before we do anything else. My hunches are usually right."

19

Almost running, Gary and Alex made their way to the IT department. Alex demanded the staff look for Nathan Lantry's use of his card or codes in the last week, and which doors he accessed. Only a few moments later, they were handed a printout of the information he requested. Giving it to Gary to figure out the door codes, Alex handed over the copy of the email about deactivating Nathan's account and then left with Gary hot on his heels.

"Are those the doors that we suspected?"

"Yes, sir. These are the doors for the main floor and the mechanical room."

"We need to get the police involved, and then we are headed straight downstairs."

There were still two officers posted at the entrance. The only reason they were still around was to keep reporters at bay. Evidently, the officer in charge had given up on looking for Liza in the building. Explaining to the officers that no one checked inside the mechanical room and that they were headed there immediately, Alex said they could call in for senior officers and stay at their post or come with them. Being rookies, they were more than happy to be involved, just in case Alex was onto something.

The four men tore down the steps, and Gary unlocked the mechanical room door. It was fairly dark, he had to use his flashlight to find the light switch. All anyone heard was the hum of the equipment. The police went forward, guns drawn. Alex lagged behind everyone else.

He stopped Gary when he noticed a door with a rug rolled up against the bottom and whispered to him.

"There's a padlock on that door. Don't you think that looks new?"

He nodded. "And it's something I won't be able to open easily. I'll call for bolt cutters." He went back to the stairwell to radio his call.

Alex waited by the closet as the police continued their search. The area was huge, and there were a lot of nooks and crannies to check to see if someone was hiding. Every so often, he could see more lights go on. Soon, Gary and another man from the maintenance department returned. The lock didn't have much room for the cutter to grab, but, eventually, they managed to cut through. The doorknob itself had been turned around, so turning the standard lock was easy. Opening the door, a whoosh of foul air hit them. Practically gagging at the smell, Alex realized Liza was on the floor curled up in a fetal position.

Gary whispered. "Is she dead?"

Alex bent down and felt for a pulse. "No, but she's in terrible shape. Call for an ambulance."

About that time, there was yelling and screaming for someone to stop, then scuffling. Alex turned back to the guard. "Quit standing there, staring, and call an ambulance. Now. We need to get her some help immediately. I'll go see if I can help the police."

Alex rushed toward the sounds of the officers, turned a corner, and practically ran into a man running full-bore. Alex knocked him to the ground, and with the police right behind him, they had the guy cuffed in no time. As they picked the guy up and brought him around the corner, the officers were surprised to see Liza in the closet.

Alex pointed to Liza. "You better call your superiors right away. They have a mess to clean up."

The officers hauled the man up the stairs while Alex and the maintenance men waited with Liza for the ambulance. Gary went to the lobby to lead the crew down and through the now-unlocked door. As far as Alex was concerned, the staff in the building were responsible for finding Liza in time. Well, he hoped it was in time. They all gave him the information he needed to find the poor woman. He asked which hospital she would be transported to, so he could notify the family to meet her there.

If only the officer had asked for the door to be unlocked in the first place, Liza may have been found on day one, instead of late in the day almost a week later. Mr. Jackson, Carolyn, and a host of other people were at the front door to thank Alex for finding her. Word that Liza was found certainly spread fast, but he was just a small cog in the wheel. They all did their part to get the job done.

As soon as Alex called Ray and Jackie, they called Cliff, while rushing to the hospital. Cliff ran out of the house toward his car, then stopped and yelled at the policeman watching him. "You can leave now. Our PI found her." He jumped in his car and slammed the door, then sped toward the hospital. He didn't care if the cop followed him or not.

Liza was in critical condition. She was treated in the emergency room upon arrival and was there for several hours. When Jackie arrived, she was the only one allowed into the emergency room to see Liza. Devastated by what she saw, Jackie reported to Ray and Cliff that Liza was on the verge of death. They all sat in the waiting room, unable to understand how Liza was in such bad shape after just a week. Now, Aaron was fussy and needed to run, but there wasn't anywhere to do so safely. Ray took him for a walk and tried to keep him happy. Giving up, he said he would take the little guy home and would come back later. Jackie's parents were on the way and would arrive in a couple of hours. Cliff paced and mumbled since that was the only way he could handle the stress he was under. He certainly didn't want to lash out at someone.

The doctors finally came out and said they couldn't tell them much this early on, but did say that Liza's condition could go either way. Cliff sat down in a corner by himself and began sobbing. Jackie joined him and the two had quite the cry fest. By the time she mopped up her tears, it was time for Liza to be transferred to the intensive care unit. They allowed Jackie to see her one more time before the move. The poor girl was so pale and fragile-looking. Jackie found a hand that was free from tubing and held on tight.

"This is Jackie. You're safe and sound now. It's time you took that independent streak of yours and used it to survive. You hear me? We're all waiting for you. Mom and Dad will be here soon too. And Cliff is out in the waiting room. Ray and Aaron went home to get a nap, but they will be back soon. You fight and pull through. Got it?" She reached down and kissed a cold cheek. Her tears plopped onto Liza's face, and she gently brushed them away. Too soon, it was time for her to leave. "I'll be back to see you as soon as they get you settled into the ICU. Fight, dear cousin. Fight."

Jackie took a good look at the monitors. She was alarmed at how low Liza's blood pressure and pulse were and shuddered before leaving the room.

Light. A soft glowing light. Liza hadn't seen light for days, and it was so peaceful. She walked toward it and could see all of her loved ones coming toward her. Her parents, brother, and Jason. Her dear husband Jason. She missed him so much. Reaching out to take his hand, her family and Jason got closer and closer. Continuing to reach out, her fingertips were all but touching Jason's.

*****

Nathan Lantry was discharged from a mental institution three weeks previous. He was still waiting for his trial date to be set on charges of assault and willful destruction of company property. His wife not only divorced him but took his family out of state. Not that he should blame her, but he did. Although clean from drugs for months now, he was still wallowing in self-pity. The apartment he was living in was far from the large fancy home he was used to.

Two weeks ago, he contacted his old dealer and began using drugs again. With limited funds, Nathan could only dabble occasionally. One day, he found his old company badge while digging through his belongings for money. He decided to see if it still worked. With no plan in mind, he walked into the building and headed straight for the stairwell. Amazingly, the door clicked open for him with a wave of his badge. He shut it behind him, let out a breath, and looked around him to see if anyone spotted his entrance. Wiping the sweat off his brow, he began trudging up the stairs to his old floor. He had to stop several times and catch his breath but finally arrived. He peeked through the glass and didn't see any movement, so he carefully opened the door to look around. With the coast clear, he wandered around the office area for a moment. The semi-darkness was somewhat creepy, but he realized that nothing had changed in the months he had been gone.

Trying to decide what his next step was going to be, he suddenly heard the elevator ping that someone had arrived. He jumped into a dark corner and crouched in the shadows. Watching as that snooty Augustine lady walked around the room, he suddenly wanted revenge. No matter that he had no dealings with her directly, he did remember that she removed Carolyn from the room that day he went berserk. She just couldn't mind her own business.

As she walked out of her office and toward the elevator bank, and before he could change his mind, Nathan grabbed her from behind and shoved her toward the stairwell. Knocking her down to the floor, he took his handkerchief and tied it around her eyes, used his belt to keep her hands behind her, and then tore part of his T-shirt to make a gag. He chuckled at his ingenuity. That's what made him good at his job. Well, his old job. Then it got taken away from him. Angry again, he forced the woman up and then told her they were going to go downstairs. Timing is everything, he thought.

When they got to the lobby landing, he realized he didn't have any place to take his hostage. They went down the final flight of stairs and to the mechanical room. The badge worked again, and inside they went. Taking a moment to adjust his eyes to the darker surroundings, he moved her forward until a closet appeared on his right. It was perfect. Someone put the doorknob on wrong, with the lock on the outside. Whoever put it on probably didn't think about the possibility of someone getting locked inside. He would have to come up with a better idea, as that lock looked fairly fragile, and he didn't want this gal to get loose. Chuckling at the mistake in his favor, he opened the closet door.

Throwing several items out of the closet, he then shoved Liza inside. Nathan locked it behind him. Now, he needed to clean up the mess, so no one would suspect anyone was in there. Gathering up the junk, he stuffed it all into a dark corner. Then he went in search of a better lock. He hated the thought of spending money on one. As he searched through old dusty cabinets and desk drawers, Nathan found rope, cleaning rags, and a brand-new padlock set. It only took a few minutes to install the lock. Feeling confident now, he left the basement through a window, so he wasn't spotted going in and out again. He certainly didn't want to be questioned. All he needed now was a fix.

The first couple of days were a no-brainer. Nathan let Liza out once a day and gave her a snack. But it became tedious, and he didn't want to mess with her anymore. Instead of letting her loose, he found a clear corner in the back of the basement where he could do his drugs and hideout. A couple of days later, he forgot about her completely. Several days after he kidnapped Liza, the lights turned on and he could hear someone walking around. He tried to hide, but there was no dark corner to sneak into. When the cops found him, he ran. But he ran right into someone and fell to the floor. As he was led right by the closet and Liza, Nathan realized he had forgotten all about her. She looked dead, and he knew things didn't look good for him now. Sitting in a cell, he finally sobered up. His lawyer wasn't going to be happy that he couldn't stay clean once he got out, and things were going to go from bad to worse if he had let that woman die. Nathan found himself in a terrible situation, made worse by his desire for drugs and a thirst for revenge.

20

Jackie entered Liza's room in the ICU every two hours on the dot. By the time her mother got there, Jackie was exhausted. Sending her home with her father to get some rest, Jackie's mother promised to talk to Liza on the same schedule and tell her not to give up. With no change in Liza's condition, and it maybe becoming even worse, Jackie was frantic for her cousin to pull through.

*****

Liza reached out for Jason, but he was suddenly gone. Eventually, he returned, and she almost touched him again. The light called to her and then sent Liza back. She was becoming frustrated because the warmth of the light was so comfortable and enticing. Yet it would suddenly disappear once again, and the darkness surrounded her. She was so tired of the dark.

*****

When Jackie returned the following morning, her mother was now exhausted. They traded off and spent the day doing much of the same thing. This went on for three days, with Liza's vitals dropping and then getting better before they finally appeared to stabilize. The doctors were now giving them hope that Liza would pull through. Cliff stopped after work each day and was always disappointed she hadn't shown any improvement. Still not allowed to visit, his frustration was building.

*****

Liza thought she heard Jackie's voice. Or was it her aunt? She wasn't sure which one. Maybe both of them. Their voices continued to tell her to fight. She wasn't sure what she was supposed to fight. She was too tired, and the darkness of the closet was awful. She didn't feel cramped anymore, though. Confusion set in, and she wished for the warm light to return.

*****

Since Liza was abducted, Cliff was acting differently from his jovial self. Very subdued, he internalized his feelings. After the police began to question his possible part in her disappearance, his emotions were all over the board. He questioned his behavior toward her before she left, and hoped she knew he loved her with all of his heart. If not, he began to think she would never know. Regrets stung, and every day he wanted to tell her how sorry he was. On the fourth day when Liza finally stabilized, he was allowed to go in for a brief visit.

Jackie took him by the arm and pulled him close to the bedside. "Talk to her, Cliff. Tell her whatever you want her to know." Then she left him alone with Liza. He stood there, scared to touch her, or say anything. His time was ticking away, and he needed to do something, or he might never get the chance.

"Liza, it's Cliff. I'm here, sweetheart. So is Jackie and her mom. They let me come visit for a couple of minutes. The doctor says you are going to make it now, but you have to keep fighting. I love you, and I need you in my life. I've missed you so much these past weeks. Please

133

come back to me, Liza. Please."

He stood and watched her still, pale body breathe. He didn't know he had reached for her hand during his little speech, but suddenly he realized how cold and lifeless Liza was. Swallowing hard, he thought that was exactly how he felt inside without her. Cold and lifeless. His visit time was up, so he bravely kissed her on the cheek, patted her hand, and not only left her room, but the hospital. When he got inside his car, he put his head into his hands and broke down crying.

*****

Liza thought she could hear Cliff's voice. The harder she listened, the surer she was. She wondered why everyone was telling her to fight. She felt different today, and Jason refused to show up again. It made her upset that the warm light wasn't there. She waited and hoped that the light and her loved ones would return for her again.

*****

Now that Liza remained stable, Jackie spent more time at home with Aaron. He was much happier now that his routine was established again. Her parents split their time at the hospital, and Jackie would pop in and out, when able. They didn't want to cause any more distress in Aaron's life, and Ray needed to go back to work. The days began to stretch out before them with little change in Liza's condition.

Even though Ray and Cliff split Alex's bill, they each added a bonus for the swift action taken. After all, if it hadn't been for Alex and his going after the answers,

Liza may not have been found for weeks or even months. The doctor said that if another couple of hours had gone by, she probably wouldn't have made it this far.

*****

Nathan Lantry was held without bond. At present, he was charged with kidnapping, along with breaking and entering, but more charges were likely to be added, once the investigation was completed. Especially since they didn't know if Liza would live or not.

Inspector Parnelli called Jackie and attempted to smooth over the mishandled case, but she didn't want to hear his lame excuses and hung up the phone. Cliff discussed the case with his lawyer, and they agreed that a different partner in the firm should handle their case. He told Cliff that they should see if there was some good that could come out of all the mistakes that were made.

Mr. Bonet took his new clients seriously. He had heard about Liza Augustine's capture but hadn't realized how complicated the case was until he sat down with Cliff and Ray. Ensconced in a conference room, the three got right down to business. Cliff wasn't comfortable in this setting and let Ray speak for them both.

"Thank you for finding the time to meet with us so soon. Liza is still unconscious in the ICU, and we haven't been given any information about how this guy captured her in the first place. Actually, outside of what our PI told us, no one is talking or giving us the facts."

"All right. Let's look over what we do know, then I'll figure out where we go from here. Let's start from the beginning where the trouble started. I have the written report from Mr. Mayfield. There was a breakdown in communication between the HR department and IT, and Mr. Lantry's ID was not deactivated in a timely manner. Is that correct?"

"Yes, that's correct. Which allowed him to access all parts of the building at any time. Someone mentioned he was going in and out of a basement window, so he wasn't spotted, but his badge still worked for the stairs and elevators if he chose to use them."

"Okay. That was mistake number one. We still don't know his motivation for taking Ms. Augustine?"

"No, we don't."

The lawyer nodded his head and made a notation. "Now we have mistake number two. The police never asked to search the mechanical room where she was found. They assumed she wasn't in there because it was a locked door."

"That's what we understand. The security guard told Alex that they were never asked to open the door for a search of the basement. Evidently, they searched every floor of the place except the basement."

"That seems a little odd, doesn't it? What was the guard's name?"

"I don't remember, but it should be in the report."

Mr. Bonet searched the document. "Ah, yes. Here it is. Gary Cooper." He highlighted the name. "Let's continue. Mr. Mayfield figured out the basement hadn't been searched and found Ms. Augustine. He talked to the right people and wasn't afraid to step on a few toes."

Cliff finally had something to say and got up the nerve to blurt it out. He jumped up from his chair and paced as he talked. "Alex saved her life. We hope. She's still very ill. We know that mistakes happen, and we aren't out to break the bank of everyone involved, but we do want accountability for Liza. Number one, the guy who kidnapped her should be thrown in jail for life for what he's done. As for her corporation, we want to make sure a process is in place, so this doesn't happen again. We know it was a random mistake, but the guy was fired for tearing up the place. Of all the people, to not deactivate..." Cliff shook his head and kept pacing. "Then he used his card for evil. Now, the police. I'm not sure where you want to go with this, but we want you to let them know that we support the department, as a whole. But as Ray, Jackie, and I will tell you, Inspector Parnelli wasted a lot of time and never followed up with his own men about no one checking out the basement, before deciding I was the guilty party. I mean, seriously." He choked up and stopped talking, then suddenly dropped into his chair.

Mr. Bonet nodded. "I understand. I will represent Ms. Augustine and the family. And, be assured, I will make sure Mr. Lantry is prosecuted. As far as her company goes, how about I send a strongly worded letter asking for proof they have completed a correction in their policy, so this doesn't happen again?" Ray and Cliff looked at each other and agreed that would be fine. "Now, what about the police?"

Ray shrugged. "Inspector Parnelli tried to apologize to Jackie, but he sounded like he was blaming everybody else for the mix-up and not taking responsibility himself. He was assigned this case, after all. And a forced apology is worthless."

"Let me do a little visiting with the police liaison, and I'll get back with you on this."

The three wrapped up their meeting, and both men felt much better now that they had representation to fight for

Liza. They drove to the hospital to check on her before they went back to work. Nothing had changed, except the doctors felt she could be moved out of the ICU in the next couple of days, as long as she remained stable.

On day nine of her hospitalization, Jackie and Ray sat down with the doctor to discuss Liza's case. "We don't understand why she is so sick or why she is still unconscious."

"When Liza was brought in, she was severely dehydrated. We did a lot of testing at that time, and because of her symptoms, we checked her blood for a variety of toxins. Especially since the man who kidnapped her was a drug addict. We weren't sure what was going on. We found some strange chemicals in her system. Nothing made any sense until someone mentioned she was found in a locked closet. We asked the building security to find out what was in there, so we could treat her appropriately. They found a can of floor stripper that wasn't sealed well, and the bottom was also rusting out. It was leaking a little bit out on the floor. Evidently, it had been there for quite some time. We believe she was breathing the fumes while locked away."

Ray nodded. "Alex said there was a terrible smell when they opened the door. And there was a rug pushed up against the bottom of the door."

"Yes, so I've heard. The nurses also scrubbed some shiny sticky stuff off her legs, so we believe it was on her skin and absorbed into her system. Chemicals affect you neurologically, and everybody reacts differently than the next person. Liza was more susceptible, in a locked closet with no airflow. We continue to wash her body out with fluids, but we also have to keep an eye on every other system. For instance, her kidneys weren't working when she came in, but they are functioning much better now.

And you've seen the heart monitors. All signs are leading to improvement each and every day. I expect she will begin to wake up any day now, but it will take her a long time to heal and build her strength back. Her body has gone through a lot of stress in the last two weeks."

"What about her mind?"

"We won't know about her speech or memory until she wakes up. We can only treat what we can medically see at this point."

"Is there anything we can do for her?"

"Not really. You talk to her, and that's good. I believe that might be the only reason she is still here. But you need to take care of yourself, too. She will need you more when she wakes up. I'll be moving her to a step-down unit tomorrow. She will still be considered critical, which means we will be monitoring her pretty much the same, but you will be able to come and go at your leisure. Also, we will have therapy come in and begin working with her muscles. Hopefully, the stimulation will help her wake up. Thankfully, she's been able to breathe on her own for the last several days. That is a good sign.

The couple left, feeling more hopeful. At least they had some answers. Jackie knew someone had tried to explain some of Liza's condition previously, but nothing soaked in because of all the stress she was under. Although in somewhat stable condition, Liza lay pale and still. The trial of Nathan Lantry would be months down the road, and their only focus would be getting Liza better in time to see him end up in jail.

21

Every day before work and right afterward, Cliff stopped by the hospital. He rarely went over to Ray's place, preferring to be alone. He talked to Liza about his day, and how he hoped she would wake up soon because they had so much to talk about.

On day twelve of her hospitalization and day eighteen from when she was kidnapped, Liza began to wake up. The physical therapist was working with her legs when he felt a twitch in her muscles. Stopping, the therapist talked to her. "Liza, if this hurts, let me know." He slowly bent her leg again, and he could see her face grimacing. Ringing for a nurse, he told her that Liza was beginning to come around, so the nurse called to inform the doctor. The therapist continued with the exercise program and talked to Liza the whole time. Her eyes began to flutter but stayed closed. By the time he was completing the assigned exercises, the doctor arrived.

"Ms. Augustine, can you hear me?" He pinched her lightly on the arm, and she jerked. "Ah. You are waking up." A nurse entered the room. "Could you shut off some of the lights, please? I don't want to blind her when I open her eyes." Soon the lights were off, and the window blinds allowed minimal lighting from the sun. "That's better. Let's take a peek, shall we?" The doctor opened one eye, then the other. "Very good, Ms. Augustine. You are in the hospital and are safe. See if you can get yourself to wake up a little more." He turned to the nurse. "You might want to call her family. If someone stays and talks to her, she might get those eyes open yet."

"Yes, Doctor."

"I'll be back to check on you, Missy. You hang in there." The room became quiet, and no one was there to see Liza raise her hand for a moment.

*****

Liza could hear someone talking, and then one of her legs hurt a little. She wasn't sure what was going on. Different voices, a moment of pain, the blasting of light in her eyes. She flinched each time. Was her captor trying to punish her? She wanted to continue to sleep or be fully awake to defend herself but couldn't figure out how to do either one. She reached up to fight off whoever was there, but she was so weak that her arm fell to her side. Then she realized it was quiet again. Thankful for the reprieve, she slipped into a deep sleep again.

*****

"Liza. Liza. Can you hear me? Come on, sweetie. You can do this. Come back to us. We need you to wake up."

Jackie talked, patted her hand, and prattled on about Aaron taking his first steps. The therapist taught her about rubbing lotion on Liza's arms and legs in a massaging manner. So, once a day, she spent time doing just that. She was talking about her mother still being at the house, and how great it was that someone was always home with Aaron. She was almost done with the massage when Liza lifted an arm. Jackie took hold of it, then leaned over in a hug.

"I'm here, Liza. I'm here. Hug me back." She felt a small pressure on her back. "Oh, Liza. Thank heavens.

Can you open your eyes? She straightened up a little to watch Liza's face. "Here. I'll get a washcloth." She prattled on as she went to the sink to warm up some water. "And the nurse left some eye drops by the bed for me to apply when I'm here. They should help your eyes feel better."

Coming back to the bedside, she washed Liza's face, paying special attention to her eyes. Then she applied the eyedrops. "Now you can try to open your eyes. I turned down the lights while I waited for the water to warm up. The nurse told me your eyes would be pretty sensitive." She sighed. "Listen to me go on and on. I'm sorry. We are all so anxious to have you open your eyes by yourself." Jackie could see her eyes flutter a bit but was unable to open them. "Squeeze my hand to let me know you hear me." Jackie could feel a little movement. "Very good, Cuz. Everyone will be so glad you're waking up."

Tears were flowing down Jackie's face, and she brushed them away with her free hand. "You work on it at your own pace. You are safe and in the hospital. They've been taking good care of you, too. The bad guy is in jail, and they aren't going to let him out on bail, either. Do you understand?" Liza gave Jackie a weak squeeze with her still-clasped hand. "Good. Once you are wide awake, we will explain everything that we know. But you rest now. We're here for you. All of us." Jackie sat with Liza for several more minutes, but she appeared to be asleep once again. "I'll be back."

Jackie sent a text to Cliff before she left the hospital to let him know that Liza was coming around slowly and to keep talking to her. He was ecstatic at the news and left work just a little earlier than usual. He didn't notice any changes, but there was at least hope. He remained several minutes longer than normal, but eventually, he gave up and left for home. Disappointment washed over him not being able to see her smile at him. All these months later, and his patience was long gone for them to be together again.

*****

Opening her eyes was so hard to do. After several attempts, she was finally able to bring a hand to her face. No blindfold, no gag. Wait. Jackie was with her at some point. Liza was in the hospital and safe. Listening, she could hear a fan blowing, doors opening and closing, and soft footsteps going by. There was some kind of noise in the room with her, and she assumed it must be equipment that she was hooked up to. The smell was definitely disinfectant, combined with something else. Was it from her hands? Raspberries? Thinking harder, she remembered Jackie telling her about how she was massaging lotion on her arms and legs. The lotion must have a raspberry fragrance. Liza relaxed. She truly was in the hospital. Someone had found her, and she was alive.

Her mind was clearing and waking up as she lay there listening. She remembered trying to reach out to Jason's hands more than once. Eventually, he went away because it wasn't her time. Tears escaped her eyes and ran down her face. She didn't have the strength to brush them away. The tears soothed her itchy, dry eyes, and she tried to open them again. Through slits, she could see her room, the doorway, and her bed. It comforted her that she was in the hospital and not dreaming. She had no idea what time it was, but it certainly was dark. Not the closet kind of darkness, though. She turned her head and could see the window. Yes. It was nighttime. Relaxing a little more, she was happy because she was safe now. She continued to work on moving her arms and legs until exhaustion set in, which didn't take long. Then she fell asleep once again.

*****

Cliff walked into Liza's room and stopped in his tracks. Propped up in bed, Liza was sitting there looking back at him. "Oh, my gosh." He practically ran to the bed and gathered her into his arms. She put her arms around him weakly. Teary-eyed, he pulled back and looked at her lovingly. "You're awake." She nodded slightly, and he frowned. "You remember me, don't you?" She nodded and gave him a weak smile. Relieved, he suddenly realized how hard he was holding Liza. "I'm so sorry. Am I hurting you?"

She whispered, "No."

"You're going to be okay now, right?"

She nodded again and whispered, "Weak."

"I'm sure." He stared at her for a long time. "Liza, I have missed you so much." She squeezed his hand a little. "I'm not sure what to do right now. You've been here a long time, and I'm so glad you're awake. Do you remember everything that happened to you?"

"Yes."

"Did he hurt you?"

"No."

"Thank heavens. I was so worried." He was sitting on the side of the bed holding Liza's hand when Jackie flew into the room.

"They said you were awake. Look at you." Cliff got

up and let Jackie have her turn hugging Liza.

Cliff stayed as long as he dared, then left for work. Jackie would remain until the nurses kicked her out to get Liza up to the shower.

"Mom will be up in a couple of hours to see you." Liza thought it would be great to see her aunt again and smiled. Talking exhausted her. Jackie was much like her mother in that way. You mostly just had to listen and reply appropriately where necessary.

*****

The shower was wonderful. Especially washing her hair more than once. Then she was put back into bed with clean sheets. She couldn't do anything for herself, but the staff was great and treated her well. After letting Liza rest for an hour, the therapist returned and began exercising her arms and legs again. No resting for her now that she had awakened. There would be a rush to get her up and around again.

After therapy, she was placed in a recliner with a small dish of Jello and a cup of ice chips at her side, neither of which held any interest to Liza. She napped until her aunt arrived. Excited to see each other, they hugged for a long time. Now her aunt was rambling on and on. Soon, Liza fell asleep, while her aunt was chatting away. When she awakened, her aunt was gone. She thought it was probably a little rude on her part, but the morning shower and therapy were very tiring. Jackie returned after lunch, and Liza hadn't touched her tray. Someone had switched out the trays with fresh items while she napped.

"Mom says you fell asleep as she was explaining an interesting story about her bridge club."

Liza chuckled. "Sorry."

"You look so much better now that you've had a shower. You smell better, too. I bet it felt good."

Liza nodded. "Exhausting."

"Are you awake enough to hear the story of my cousin who got abducted?"

"Yes."

"Good. But you have some fresh Jello sitting here. I'm going to feed you while I tell the story."

She grimaced. "Not hungry."

"Technically, it's fluid, so deal with it. Here we go."

Liza opened her mouth and took her first bite, as Jackie began the tale of what happened once she was taken. She explained about the fiasco with the police inspector, and how Ray hired a PI to find her. Liza was certainly curious how they found her. It was upsetting to find out that they could have found her so much sooner, possibly that first day, had the police searched the mechanical room. The Jello was long gone, but Jackie was still talking and had switched over to spooning ice chips into her mouth. Liza had to admit the cold felt good melting down her parched throat.

"So, anyway, you didn't wake up until during the night or early morning on day thirteen. I guess it would be Lucky Thirteen. The day before, you started twitching and stuff, so we were all hoping it would happen right away, but you waited until nobody was around."

"Cliff."

"What about him?"

"How did he handle me missing?"

"Not well. Especially after Inspector Parnelli tried to accuse him of kidnapping you and hiding your body." Liza closed her eyes and shook her head. "Liza, while

146

you were in France, did you make a decision about him?"

"When I was in the closet."

Jackie's eyes widened. "The closet? Not until then?"

Liza felt almost ashamed of pushing Cliff into the background. "Too busy."

"Liza." Jackie's breath whooshed out. "What was your decision?"

Before she could answer, Cliff came into the room. He bent down, kissed Liza, and gave her an awkward hug. Jackie was disappointed that she didn't get to hear the answer to her question and sighed.

"I'll leave you two alone. Liza, I'll stop in the morning. I'll give Aaron a kiss from you.

"Thanks for everything."

When Jackie left, Liza took Cliff's hand and told him to sit down. "How are you?" she squeaked out.

"I'm better now that you are awake. I've missed you so much."

"Me, too. I can't talk much. Hold me."

Cliff was glad to comply and scooted his chair toward her so they could hug. The longer he held her, the better she felt. She tried to reciprocate, but her arms still didn't have much strength. They both cried happy tears, and it was a special moment for them.

"Did Jackie tell you everything about trying to find you?" She nodded. "Did you have any questions?"

"Not really."

"Then let me tell you about hiring a lawyer." She nodded again and waved her hand for him to go ahead. "Mr. Bonet is someone that was recommended to me by my personal lawyer. Ray and I hired him to help get Nathan Lantry prosecuted to the fullest extent possible. But besides all of that, we want him to make sure your company fixes its process so that individual badges or codes no longer work the day they leave the building." Liza raised her eyebrows in alarm.

"Not suing, just a request by a letter."

"Oh, okay."

"The other is a more delicate matter, and I'm not sure how it will be handled yet. The police screwed up by not asking for access to check the mechanical room. Evidently, there is more to the building than meets the eye. The door states it is the mechanical room, but there is a whole basement under there that is not being used, except for a little storage. Nathan found himself a little corner to hide in and do drugs. The cops found all kinds of paraphernalia, along with blankets, a pillow, and some dirty clothes. I don't know if he was actually living down there or what. We haven't gotten all the details yet. Anyway, if they had just gone through the door right away and done a complete search, you probably would have been found a few hours after your abduction. Instead, our private investigator and one of the security guards he was working with found you. They took two rookie policemen with them, and they were the ones that found Nathan. We want accountability, and I want a pound of flesh from Inspector Parnelli."

Liza patted Cliff's hand, then laid her head back. "I'm tired."

He hugged her again, followed by a soft kiss. "I'll be back tomorrow. When do you start therapy?"

Grimacing, Liza said, "I already have, and they'll be back in a few minutes."

"I'll let you rest, then. I love you."

"Love you, too." Closing her eyes, she was asleep before Cliff went through the door.

Within a few days, Liza was moved to a rehab unit. Her family and friends could visit anytime, but most of her days were spent rebuilding her muscles. Jackie's mom went home after having stayed a month, and Jackie would visit at night, once Ray was home from work. She didn't stay long, as Liza was always worn out from rehab all day. Liza's voice was getting stronger, along with her arms and legs. Her appetite was increasing, too. After a couple of weeks, she could eat more than a piece of toast. Her body was craving calories now that she was in rehab. She frequently had protein shakes or smoothies as they went down much easier than regular food. She was determined to get strong enough to be discharged home. It had been months since she had seen the inside of her apartment. She had forgotten about her suitcase and purse left in the ride share, but Jackie eventually retrieved it all from the police once she was found. She brought Liza her phone and charger when she was finally strong enough to use it.

Mr. Jackson stopped to see her a couple of times. Jackie promised to tell him when she could receive visitors, so it was good to see him again. The second time Liza was much more alert, and they discussed the division in France. He reassured Liza that it was still getting along fine, and Pierre was given a new position due to his hard work in his attempts to save the company. He was now a vice-president, very much like her job. She was pleased with the news and knew that Felicia would be immensely proud of her husband. But she also chuckled because Pierre refused the position several times, before finally accepting the much-deserved promotion.

Carolyn stopped by and thanked her profusely for the

gifts. Liza laughed at her story of keeping them out of the officer's hands so they couldn't be smudged up while he was looking for fingerprints. Mrs. Carney and Casey each stopped by once. The room was full of flowers from friends, now that she wasn't in the ICU anymore. When one bunch was ready to be tossed, another would arrive to take its place. It seemed as if she was living in a flower shop.

Overall, Cliff and Liza developed a new bond. When she got strong enough to have a serious conversation, she admitted to her fears of losing another husband. But along the way, she almost lost her life, instead. One never knows, and they needed to love each other to the fullest while they had the chance. He felt the same way, realizing he could have lost Liza just as easily and would have regretted not having loved her more. They both had their reasons for hesitating, but they were beyond that now. They came to the conclusion they now had more respect for each other as they moved through her illness. Their relationship was being built on a whole different plane. When Liza thought about it, she figured it was because of their maturity and life experiences under their belts. Not like the young love that she and Jason had.

22

A little over two months from when Liza woke up, she was walking with a walker or a cane and was able to dress herself again. Considering how sick and as close to death she had been, it was quite an accomplishment. The therapy team was talking about her discharge happening in a few days, but Liza had a few questions that needed to be answered before she walked out those doors. Having requested to see the neurologist, Liza was told to expect him the following day.

"Ms. Augustine, it's very good to see your progress to the point of going home. I wanted to make sure I followed up with you, anyway, so I'm glad you had them call me in."

"I'm thrilled to get this far myself, Dr. Zinner."

"What can I do for you? They reported that you had some questions."

"I understand I was exposed to a chemical, which caused me to deteriorate faster than I would have otherwise."

"Yes, I was a little confused when you were brought in. When I was told you were taken by a drug user, we checked your bloodwork for those types of substances, thinking he may have drugged you. But nothing showed up in your system. Then someone mentioned that you were being held in a basement closet, so I had someone check to see what chemical might have been inside with you. A can of floor stripper wasn't quite tight, and the bottom had rusted out. It was leaking the contents onto the floor, so, subsequently, you ended up with some on your legs. You were also inhaling the fumes. Being in a closed space just made it worse."

"What's in the stripper?"

"Ammonia, which I'm sure you are familiar with. But other caustic substances are included to break down the old floor wax. You can imagine what it would do if a person inhaled it for a long time. Between your constant breathing of poisonous air and getting it on your skin, it adversely affects your organs and nervous system. There were some chemical burns on your legs that the nurses washed off, but I believe the wounds healed up nicely once you were treated. It helped that you were wearing a pair of jeans, to keep the worst from touching your skin. I suggest you try to never be around those types of cleaning products again. Your sensitivity to them is off the charts. Of course, this product was for office buildings, so it's not like you can buy it off the shelf for home. But you can purchase straight ammonia, and I don't recommend it at all."

"Don't use ammonia products. Got it. So, being exposed to this stuff made my organs shut down and my muscles weak?"

"Yes. I was initially surprised by how it affected your nervous system so quickly until the information came through you were in that closet. It explained why you were comatose, and then your organs and muscles began to deteriorate. Everything works together, so if one begins to fail, it all falls like dominoes."

"I see. Do you think I'll ever be one hundred percent again? After all, I almost died."

"I believe so. Certainly. Most of your weaknesses will be improved rapidly. Nothing was working and now everything is. I mean, you weren't even eating and drinking. But look at you. You're beginning to fill out your clothes and that's a good thing. Besides, your mind works just fine. What a blessing."

"It is."

And just like that, a couple of days later, Liza was standing in her living room. Jackie had Aaron with her, and he was enjoying the open space. So many things to check out with his little fingers. Jackie had a cleaning lady come and spruce up the place for Liza but made sure she didn't use any ammonia products to clean with. The place smelled clean and fresh. Her refrigerator was filled with fresh fruits and vegetables. Even some frozen treats were tucked away. Using only her cane, Liza walked around her apartment and took some deep breaths. She was almost overwhelmed being home again. About six months from the time she left for France, Liza walked back through the door. So much happened in that time. She turned back to Jackie and reached out for a hug. Liza was so happy to be home again.

Soon, she was alone in her thoughts. Continuing to explore her apartment, it was almost like the first day she moved in a couple of years previous. Peace surrounded her. Smiling, she texted Cliff to have him come over. After all, it was Wednesday, and they needed to go to Charlie's.

Cliff fussed over her as they left her apartment, trying to help her with walking. She had an elevator and didn't need to take the stairs like she used to. They were both excited about going to supper together, but what surprised them both was when they walked in, Liza got a standing ovation from the staff. While it was heartwarming, it was also embarrassing at the same time. The other customers had no clue what was going on. Several weeks previous, Cliff stopped by one evening after work and told the staff about Liza being injured. When she called him to come over, he gave the café a quick call to let them know they would both be in that evening, so their table was open and waiting for them. The staff were excited to have them return, and the couple appreciated them wholeheartedly.

Liza still wasn't eating a full meal, but she did order a simple hamburger with no fries and a shake. Liquid was easier for her to get her calories. The couple had a great evening, and she felt more normal than ever. Charlie's staff refused to let them pay for their meals that evening, and the couple thanked them profusely. The staff yelled, "See you next Wednesday," as they walked out the door.

Exhausted by the time she got back to the apartment, Liza was ready to call it a night. Cliff left her resting on the couch yawning and slipped out the door. Waiting for a moment, she then locked up and went to bed. Being in her own bed again meant normalcy. She hadn't slept that well in weeks, awakened refreshed, and realized she smelled coffee. When Liza finally reached the kitchen, she found a fresh pot of coffee already brewed. Jackie bought her a new maker with a timer. Her old one had gone on the fritz months ago. What a great gift to wake up to.

Taking her time, she ate a little breakfast, took a shower, and put on some casual, comfy clothes. Everything was still a little big for her, but she would eventually gain back some weight. Jackie would be picking her up later that morning for therapy. She planned to run some errands before returning to the rehab center to pick up Liza. They were both happy they didn't have to go inside a hospital again. For the next couple of weeks, Jackie would be taking Liza back and forth to her therapy appointments. She honestly thought if she began walking in the park again, it would do her more good than anything else. Liza talked it over with her therapists and they thought it was a great idea, but hoped she would take someone with her in case she did too much or had a fall. They knew Liza well enough to know she would push her limit. On the way home, she asked Jackie about going with her.

"Great idea. Let's do it on opposite days of therapy. I don't think you can do them both on the same day. I can push Aaron in the stroller, too. We should have enough pleasant weather left to get your strength built back up."

"Wonderful. Call me before you come over. I'll be waiting. Oh. I forgot to mention, I have a follow-up appointment with my doctor next week, right after therapy. He's going to let me know when I can go back to work. I'll need to be able to drive, so it will be up to therapy to decide if I'm strong enough and have good enough reflexes."

"Getting bored already?"

"Not necessarily bored, but my brain needs the stimulation. I've been working so hard on my body; my brain feels a little mushy."

"Mushy?"

"Yeah." She chuckled. "That's a good word for it, I think."

The following week, Liza was discharged from therapy, but she was to keep up walking in the park or on a treadmill. The park trail was perfect to hike and build up her muscles. Plus, the crisp fall air was invigorating. The doctor released her to go to work the following week, and that gave Liza time to prepare. She needed to make sure she woke up earlier since she moved so much slower. Calling Mr. Jackson, Liza was happy to find out that he was looking forward to her return. Projects were backed up. She promised to bring in the appropriate paperwork from the doctor to show that she was released.

Every day, Liza worked on getting herself ready in the mornings. She had been laid back for so long that it took her a little while to get things done quicker. Cliff made sure the car started and had a full tank of gas. She felt prepared by Sunday night, but Monday morning brought self-doubt. She managed to get to work on time, but just barely. Carolyn, Mr. Jackson, and Casey were all waiting for her at the elevator. The other staff stood in their doorways. The office welcomed her home, and it was a good feeling.

Liza left her cane in her car, hoping she didn't have to do much walking on her first day back. With Liza making her way to her office, Mr. Jackson and Carolyn followed her, while everyone else drifted off. Her desk held balloons and cupcakes as a welcoming gift. She almost cried.

"Thank you so much. I've missed everyone. I didn't realize how much until I stepped off the elevator."

"We've missed you, too. I knew you'd want to get right to work, so Carolyn has a file on her desk when you are ready. I figured you needed something easy and straightforward to start with."

"Unlike the project you handed me when I took this job."

"Correct. Welcome home." He grinned, then left the room, while Carolyn rushed over and hugged Liza.

"I'm so glad you're back. Nothing has been the same without you. When you need a break this week, I want you to tell me all about France."

"You got it." Liza made her way to her desk chair. "You better share the cupcakes with everyone."

"You bet."

Carolyn left one cupcake on the corner of the desk by the balloons and took the rest to hand out to the other staff. Liza sat back and looked around. Nothing had changed, except her. She always valued everybody else's life, but now she valued her own. No one knew better than her how short life could be. She had been taught that repeatedly. *"You'd think I'd learn."* Shaking her head, she decided to get to work.

Liza spent the morning answering emails. One from the IT department jogged her memory. It described the new provision for disabling passwords, badges, and codes when a person was no longer employed by the company. After testing the process several times, they believed it improved and strengthened the safety features which she had requested. Cliff mentioned something about that a long time ago. She replied with a polite "thank you", and that, since this was her first day back, she hoped her lawyer had been contacted with the information and appreciated them notifying her about the results.

Rubbing her tired eyes, Liza turned her chair toward the window and closed them to rest for a few minutes. Almost dozing off, she heard a knock on the door. Turning back around, she saw Casey standing in the doorway.

"Come on in."

"I didn't want to disturb you."

"I was resting my eyes. I'm not used to all of this computer work."

"I've got just the thing. A weak pair of readers. Now that I have bifocals, I never use them. I'll bring them with me to work tomorrow."

"Do you think that they will help?"

"I bet they will. They magnify the words so you don't

have to strain your eyes, and it will be easier for you to read that way. All this paperwork would make anyone's eyes go bonkers."

"Sure. I'll try them."

"Great. The reason I stopped by was I have a proposition for you."

"Oh, yeah?"

"Yeah. I buy you lunch, and you help me figure out this issue I have with my current project."

"I'd love to. I still don't have a great appetite, but a fruit smoothie and half of a chicken sandwich from the cafeteria will be fine."

"You got it. I'll be back soon, and we will chat about France over lunch."

"Don't tell Carolyn. She's been waiting for months to talk about France." They both laughed after they heard Carolyn complain from the other room about them talking about France without her.

Liza turned her chair back around and closed her eyes again. Eye drops would be just the ticket about now. She spent fifteen minutes resting, then turned back to her desk. She already addressed everything that needed to be done that morning. The only thing left was the file folder Mr. Jackson wanted her to look through. She dreaded touching it because she didn't know whether she was ready or not to approach the analytical side of things. Before she reached for it, Casey arrived.

They shut the door and laughed way too much over lunch. Then they concentrated on the problem at hand and felt they found the perfect solution by the time they were done. Liza was grateful that her brain could still problem-solve and calculate figures with accuracy. No amount of physical therapy could help her brain, but working with Casey was therapy of its own. She felt like she could now approach that file on her desk with confidence.

Two hours later, she took the file and a stack of notes out to Carolyn. "Please see this all gets to Pete for me."

"Would you like me to type up your notes?"

"No. He's used to reading my scribbles. Make a copy for me is all. If he has any questions, he can call me or stop by. I'm leaving for home a little early."

"Good. You've worked hard today."

Liza grabbed her purse and headed for the elevator. By the time she got to her car, exhaustion had taken over. She had done way too much, and she couldn't wait to get home. She peeled off her work clothes, put on her jammies, and collapsed in her recliner. She was awakened by insistent knocking on her door.

"Who is it?" she yelled out.

"Cliff."

"Just a minute."

She sat up and stretched, then realized it was dark. Not only inside her apartment but outside as well. Unlocking the door, she let Cliff come in. She switched on a light, and he looked at her oddly.

"Did I get you out of bed?"

"No." She yawned. "My chair."

"I'm sorry. I was going to see if you wanted me to bring over supper, but your phone was off again."

"Bad habit when I'm at work."

"How about I bring you a malt?"

"That would be great. One more thing. Could you stop at a drugstore or somewhere that sells eyedrops? I need something for dry eyes."

"Sure. I'll be back in a jiffy."

"I'll leave the door unlocked."

Blessedly, Cliff found the eyedrops, and Liza put them in immediately upon his return to the apartment. She couldn't believe how much better her eyes felt after just a couple of minutes. They talked about their day while he ate, and she sipped her malt.

"You'll have a better day tomorrow, and each day will continue to get easier."

"I hope so." She yawned again.

"You better go to bed. I'll call you tomorrow. That is, if your phone is on."

"I'll turn it on right now. You get out of here. I need my beauty sleep."

"No, you don't. You are beautiful already." He kissed her soundly before scooting out the door.

When she sat down at her desk the following morning, a pair of rhinestone pink reading glasses were waiting for her. She couldn't help laughing but put them on and checked herself out in the mirror. They were fabulous, and she did find that they helped her read easily. The eyedrops were helping, too. She stopped by Casey's office later that morning.

Flipping the glasses around by the bow, she said, "These are crazy looking. Where did you get them?"

"Oh, one of those Bohemian places I love to shop at." Casey always dressed in flowing outfits that had rhinestones, beads, or sequins. Sometimes all three. Even her business attire was far from sedate.

"You know, if I tried to dress like you, everyone would think I was headed to a costume party. But you carry it off like nobody's business. You make me jealous."

Casey stood up and showed off her latest outfit. "I've

always dressed like this, so no one pays any attention to me anymore. Why not try a wilder look? Maybe change your blouses to some hot colors or a wild print under that bland jacket of yours."

Liza shook her head. "I like blending in with the crowd. It's safer there. See, if I robbed a bank, no one would be able to describe me. You, on the other hand, would stick out like a sore thumb." They both chuckled at the image she created. "Anyway, I wanted to check to see if our little chat solved your problem."

"Perfectly. We are on a roll now. Say, you look like you feel better today."

"I never feel bad, just tire easily. But it helps to go home early. I'm trying not to push it, but I feel guilty leaving everyone slaving away while I nap in my recliner."

"I'm sure you do." Casey stuck out her tongue. "If there is anything I can do, let me know."

"You bet. And thanks again for the glasses."

Heading down to the cafeteria, Liza picked out something for lunch. Trying to eat healthy foods and increase her intake was a daily battle. She needed to prove to her doctor she could regain more weight, and she needed the calories to continue to heal. Instead of going back to her office like she usually did, Liza found a table where she could look out into the back garden. The wind was blowing too hard for her to enjoy sitting outside in the sunshine. She was daydreaming when a voice interrupted her thoughts.

"Ms. Augustine?"

She turned and saw a security guard standing by her table. "Yes."

"I thought it was you. My name is Gary Cooper. I

helped Mr. Mayfield find you."

"Sit down and join me. I'm done eating, and you can have my table." He smiled shyly and set his tray down. When he was settled, Liza said, "Thank you for finding me."

"Mr. Mayfield asked all the right questions to the right people. I was only there to assist. But I wanted to tell you how good you look and that I'm glad we found you in time. I have to say, I wasn't sure you were alive when we opened that closet." He shook his head. "I had nightmares until they told me you were going to make it."

She reached over and patted his hand. "Thank you for your assistance. I was in terrible shape. There was a chemical leaking onto the floor and that was what made me so sick." She took a deep breath and slowly released it. "Mr. Cooper, whatever your part in finding me was, I appreciate it more than you know."

"I'm glad to see you back at work. I will sleep better now."

She looked at his tray of food. "You better get busy eating, or your food will get cold. Thank you for stopping to say hello."

"My pleasure, Ma'am. It was good to see you again and thank you for inviting me to sit with you."

"Anytime." Liza got up to leave, then extended her hand to shake his. Changing her mind, she bent over to give him a big hug instead.

As she rode the elevator back up to her floor, she thought about her kidnapping. It was truly a miracle that she was alive, but she still didn't know why Nathan took her in the first place.

23

The first three days after he was caught, Nathan felt very confined in the jail cell. Of course, he needed to come down off all of his drugs, so everything bothered him. The itch to get more was always there, but now he was stuck. He was held under close observation at first, and his paranoia was off the charts. Now that he had sobered up, the jailers moved him to a different cell. He was just a little bit scared of the other inmates and tried to keep to himself as much as possible.

His trial date for the first offense arrived, and he was given six months of incarceration along with probation upon his release. But with his recent antics, Nathan assumed he wouldn't see the light of day for years. The new trial was long after his current sentence, so he was hoping to be released for a few weeks while he waited. But that wasn't to be. When he went to court for his initial hearing for kidnapping Liza, the judge denied bail. Looking around the tight cell where he was spending his time, Nathan knew he was going to need something to keep his mind busy. Eventually, he asked his lawyer to find him some decent reading material instead of the worn-out paperbacks available from the jail library. The lawyer came through, got him a card from the local library, and checked out several books for him. He even made arrangements that someone from the library would come to the jail every two weeks and trade out the books for him.

Because he wasn't technically a dangerous man, he was given a few more privileges than some of the troublemakers. One was being able to meet the librarian in the facility library to exchange books. He got to know Sarah, and they talked about the books he was reading. Surprised she was reading the same genre, they hit it off and began to have personal conversations. He discussed his past marriage and was open and honest about why his wife left and took his family away from him. Sarah encouraged Nathan to join the AA group that was held in the jail every week. Up until then, he had refused to consider joining any group at any time. Even when his wife implored him to get clean, and his lawyer was trying to get him a lesser sentence.

The half-hour he spent with Sarah twice a month was good therapy, and he complimented her on her ability to help him work through his feelings. Sarah admitted that she was almost out of college with a degree in psychology and was currently working on her thesis. Nathan encouraged her to practice on him as long as she wanted because she was very good.

Four months after Nathan was arrested for the kidnapping charge, his lawyer arrived to see him. They went over step-by-step what he had done, and thankfully, the woman was still alive. Otherwise, a murder rap would have meant a life sentence. Preparing for his court case brought up a lot of feelings that he had pushed down. He was still upset about his firing, even though he knew it was his fault. Sarah tried to get him to forgive his wife for leaving and taking his family with her, but there was something deep inside of Nathan that wouldn't let the anger go. His lawyer told him if he didn't take full responsibility for his actions, the sentence was going to be much longer, and he was in deep trouble as it was.

Mr. Bonet asked to help prosecute Nathan Lantry and

joined the team that would be handling the case. He promised the family that the man would pay for his crimes and planned to see this case through. Several months went by before he set up an appointment to meet with Liza Augustine and her family. He wanted to make sure he had all the facts in front of him beforehand. They arranged to meet at his office one afternoon and were all seated around the conference table. Even Aaron was happily eating some Cheerios as the adults conversed.

"As you already know, Mr. Lantry was denied bail. He is currently serving a six-month term for the incident at the office but will not be released when that term is up."

Liza frowned. "I hope not."

"He didn't make it more than a couple of weeks the last time he was on his own, so the courts didn't believe it would be safe to release him to await trial this time, either."

Cliff butted in. "Did he ever say why he kidnapped Liza?" He reached over, took her hand, and held on tight.

"That's the thing. He had no excuse or reason. He was there, she was there, and it just happened."

Liza sat up straight. "What do you mean? What was he doing there in the first place?"

Mr. Bonet cleared his throat. "Let me start over. Mr. Lantry was released from a halfway house and was renting a small apartment to live in until he went to his original court hearing. He wasn't sure about the timeline, but a week or so later, he found his old dealer and began to purchase small amounts of drugs. With little money to his name by this point, he stated he couldn't buy as much as he wanted. One day, he found his old company badge, and on a whim, decided to try it out. Since it worked, he went up to his old office and was standing there trying to figure out what he wanted to do while there. He didn't have a plan in place, since he was surprised he could still get in after all those months. All he could say was that he was mad at being fired, and was trying to decide what to do when Liza walked in. He heard the elevator, so he hid in a corner and watched. When he realized it was her, he thought about how she had rescued the secretary that day he was throwing files around, so he grabbed her from behind. We all know he made you go down the stairs, but when he got to the main floor, he knew then that there was no place else to go but down another flight. His badge allowed him into the basement, and he eventually made a little home for himself back in some dark corner to do his drugs."

The lawyer cleared his throat again and took a drink. "Putting Liza in a closet was done on a whim. But I would say it was all deliberately done to keep her quiet. Mr. Lantry admitted he forgot about Liza after a couple of days because he was high on drugs and that was all he could think about. After his arrest, when he walked by the closet and saw her on the floor, he realized what he had done. He figured you were dead, and he was in big trouble. So, that's the gist of it."

Liza thought Cliff was going to crush her hand, so she extricated it carefully. "Basically, no plan and no premeditation."

"Correct."

Jackie allowed the conversation to play out as she continued to keep Aaron occupied, but she had heard enough. "You will make sure he will spend time for kidnapping, though, right?"

"Yes. As far as Liza goes, kidnapping is our best bet. He didn't mean to leave her in a closet to die, and he had no idea about the chemical attempting to kill her off. Had that can of stripper not been in there, she would have been in fairly decent shape once the door was opened. What I'm saying is, there was no intent to kill Liza. And there wasn't really any intent to harm her, either. In his short-sighted thinking, it was a punishment of sorts, and he was just trying to get even."

Liza got up and stretched. "Just talking about that closet makes me hurt. Will there be anything else, Mr. Bonet? I trust you will do the right thing."

He stood up, followed by everyone else in the room. "Like I said before, I'll do my best. After I talked to the rest of the prosecuting team, we are sure he will be in jail for quite some time. There are other charges, of course, but they aren't related to you personally."

Liza gave him a curt nod. "Thank you, but I need a bit of fresh air." She turned and left the room, Cliff running after her.

Ray spoke up. "I think the closet still haunts her. Will she need to be at the trial?"

"Yes. But we can arrange for her to be there only for the time she is scheduled to tell her story, so she doesn't have to listen to everything else."

"I think that is best, don't you Jackie?" He reached over to take Aaron.

"Yes. We haven't talked about it much since her release from the hospital. Her focus has been on rebuilding her strength and getting her life back on track."

"I will sit with her before the trial and discuss her lengthy rehabilitation. That will be necessary to bring up in court to show how much damage he did to her physically by kidnapping her. It's much harder to prove the damage mentally, but right there shows you that she is still suffering when I mentioned the closet. She will probably have severe claustrophobia from here on out."

Jackie nodded. "Liza hasn't mentioned nightmares, but it wouldn't surprise me. Cliff hasn't said anything either. I'm not sure they talk about the incident. All I know is that he wants to marry her but feels that he should wait until the trial is over before they talk about their future plans."

"A person has to heal in their own time. You can't rush these things. Many times, once the trial is over, the victim has closure and can go on with their life. She may need that. You certainly know her better than I do."

Ray reached over to shake Mr. Bonet's hand. "Thank you for your time. We appreciate the explanation, and we will be there for Liza, whatever she needs."

Mr. Bonet walked them out and they joined Cliff and Liza on the sidewalk in front of the office. Liza reached out to Jackie and gave her a quick hug.

"Sorry. I had to get out of there. Things aren't any easier to talk about now as they were a few months ago."

"Not a problem. You talk when you need to. All of us are here for you. Mr. Bonet said that he would meet with you closer to the trial date and go over everything then. Just you and him. Will you be okay with that?"

"I have to be. I want to make sure Nathan is thrown in jail for what he did to me."

"Okay. Let's all get some ice cream." Aaron's eyes lit up and clapped his hands, then everyone chuckled.

Liza grinned. "That sounds like a great plan to me."

24

After the meeting at Mr. Bonet's office, all of the memories from the kidnapping loomed large. Liza couldn't get it out of her mind, and the nightmares began again. Not only was she dreaming about the closet, but about her parents, brother, and Jason. Of course, the dreams were convoluted, and none of them made any sense. But as the weeks continued, they only became worse and more horrific. Cliff noticed first, and she tried to wave off the concerns. But she couldn't fool him. They were too close now to pull the wool over his eyes. Then Carolyn asked what the problem was.

"Ms. Augustine, are you sick again? You look like you are ill. Similar to when you first came back to work."

"I'm fine. Really. I haven't been sleeping well the last couple of weeks, that's all. Too much going on around here, I guess."

Carolyn gave Liza a strange look but shrugged her shoulders. "Let me know if there is anything you need."

"Thank you, Carolyn. I appreciate you keeping an eye on me."

Liza went back to her desk, then stood right back up to go look in the mirror. She looked awful. Carolyn was right. There were bags under her eyes, her face had a strained look, and a permanent frown was in place. She couldn't deny the fact that she was in trouble again. Now, with Cliff and Carolyn noticing, she knew they would be watching her closely. All she needed was Jackie to start in and that would complete the picture. She sighed, then closed the door to her office so she could make a call in private.

The doctor wouldn't be available for a few days, but Liza made the earliest appointment she could get to see him. She did ask for a call back if he had a cancellation, as it was rather urgent. In the meantime, she needed to buck up and get a grip on her life again. The fall weather had turned wet and rainy, which kept her from the park trails, but she vowed to use the treadmill in the apartment complex as soon as she got home. It wouldn't take much to wear her out. Maybe then she could sleep. The day finally arrived for her appointment, and she left work early. She told Carolyn that she probably wouldn't return. That didn't help Carolyn not to fret over her.

"Dr. Moline, thank you for seeing me again."

"I looked at your hospital records. It sounds like you have had quite an ordeal to overcome again."

"Yes. And this time, things have escalated into terrible nightmares. I had a few while I was in the hospital, but they eventually went away. They were nothing like what

I'm experiencing now or in the past."

"When did they start?"

Thinking back, she replied, "Right after we visited with the lawyer about the upcoming trial. When we have an actual court date, I will have to go over all of the trauma I experienced to prepare for my part of the trial."

"Can you tell me a little bit about the dreams?"

"They vary from person to person, but they are becoming more horrific as the days go by. Like my parents. If you remember, I found them in their bed." The doctor nodded. "Well sometimes the house is on fire, and we're all caught in the flames and I'm trying to rescue them. Or my brother might be in the same fire and he's trying to help me." She took a breath and tried to continue, but her voice caught with emotion.

"I see. How about your husband? Is he anywhere in these dreams?"

She nodded. Dr. Moline set a box of tissues by her side as she answered his question. "I see him, along with all the other cars, in mangled piles of steel. He's calling out to me for help, but I'm just standing there asking him what to do. I'm helpless to save him."

"And the kidnapping?"

Shaking her head, she began to stare at the floor. Clutching the tissues in her hands, she practically ripped them to shreds. "That's what's so weird. I seldom dream about the closet."

"Hmmm. That is odd. I know you have been doing well until the time of your kidnapping, but I assume that you need therapy to help you sort through all of this. In the past, Jackie has helped you, but she isn't trained, and this sounds like some unresolved issues that need professional help."

Taking a deep breath, Liza looked at the doctor. "You know I hated all those people. They wanted to drug me and commit me. I'm not willing to do that again. That's why I came to see you."

Dr. Moline gave her a gentle smile and patted her hand. "Let's do this. I'd like to restart your anti-depressant at a low dose, and after the trial, maybe we can wean you off like we did the last time."

"What about the counseling you think I need?"

"I have someone who I believe can help. She doesn't live around here but is available to meet with you over the computer."

"A Zoom call with a therapist?"

"Yes. It's technically called "telehealth". Would that be an option for you?"

"What makes her so special from others I've seen?"

"She handles traumatic cases. Sometimes things that happen in the now bring up trauma from the past. I believe you qualify for her therapy."

"And you trust her?"

"I do, or I wouldn't have suggested her, would I? Now, what do you say?"

"I can try and see how it goes."

"I believe that would be best. I will put in the referral and someone from her office will call you to set up a time. In the meantime, you get started on the prescription I am sending down to the pharmacy. And while you are there, you might pick up some melatonin to help you rest at night. I'm not saying it will help but give it a try."

"Sure, I can do that."

"Now, on another note, I see you are losing weight again. Are you not eating?"

"When I was in the hospital, I lost about twenty pounds. I gained ten of that back before discharge and was working on the other ten. My appetite hasn't been very good since my illness, but I'm trying. Then these nightmares started, and I lost my appetite again. I drink shakes and smoothies a lot."

"That concerns me, too. You need more proteins and less fat content than ice cream offers. While you are at the pharmacy, pick up some protein drinks or powders. If solid food isn't going down, you need to take in some type of protein and vitamins. I see you are still taking your daily supplements."

Cringing, Liza replied, "Well, not really. I have them in the house, but I haven't been good about taking them the last few weeks."

"Young lady, you need to get back on them right

away. Are you still walking?"

"I try to fit that in. Honest. The weather has been too awful to walk outside, but I have been going to the gym at the apartment to walk on the treadmill instead. It certainly isn't near as fun."

"No, I imagine not. Okay. Let's see. I ordered your medication, and here is a list of things I want you to pick up while you are at the pharmacy. Then, before you leave, make a follow-up appointment with me in the next two or three weeks and I'll see how you are doing. I'll get that referral off to Dr. Peachtree and someone will contact you from her office. Is there anything else we need to cover today?"

"Dr. Peachtree. That's quite a name."

"Believe me. She is a peach."

"One more thing. My lab work hasn't been drawn since I left the hospital. Do you think there is anything that I should have redone? Especially since I haven't been eating very well."

"Let me see. I looked over the earlier results and didn't notice anything special. Maybe we should check to see if you are anemic. Chemicals in your bloodstream could have that effect on you and might be long-lasting. It doesn't look like they checked that before your dismissal. Let's do that, and since the lab will be drawing anyway, well just check on other things while we are at it." The doctor typed away for a minute. "Okay. Orders are in for everything. You can run down to the lab before you leave. Don't forget to make your follow-up appointment on the way out. I'll have someone call you with the results of your labs either way."

"Thank you, Dr. Moline. I appreciate everything you've done for me."

"Anytime, Ms. Liza. I'll see you in a couple of weeks."

Liza left the clinic, making her next appointment on her way out. Dr. Moline always made her feel better emotionally. A huge weight was off her shoulders and she headed toward the lab. She hoped that Dr. Peachtree could help her. Heading to the pharmacy, Liza knew that drugs weren't the answer, but the anti-depressants had helped in the past and had no qualms about starting them again. She took the folded paper out of her purse that Dr. Moline had given her with the list of items he wanted her to pick up. She read down the list. Prescription, melatonin, multi-vitamins, and laugh and smile. With a smiley face drawn at the bottom, she couldn't help but smile and chuckle at Dr. Moline's note. What a guy.

Four days later, Dr. Peachtree's office called and set up a time for later that afternoon. Liza was still at work and wondered if she should leave or just shut her door for the duration of the call. Since it was going to be the initial visit, she decided the workplace would be fine. Not sure about the additional appointments, though, she planned to ask. As three-thirty rolled around, she shut her door after telling Carolyn she would be indisposed for a meeting online. Dr. Peachtree and Liza spent their half-hour introducing themselves and visiting about how she would proceed with treatment. Liza was in awe of the woman already. She was professional, yet personable. Liza felt very comfortable talking to her. She hoped that this therapist would continue to be so because many of them were condescending and impatient with her in the past.

When she closed out of their session, Liza couldn't wait to have her next visit with the doctor. Dr. Peachtree believed that Liza should not be at work during her appointments, even if she was taking a lunch break. They arranged their next session at four, and Liza planned to leave early that day.

The melatonin was helping Liza get more rest, but she was also working out like a demon in the evenings. When both Cliff and Carolyn mentioned she was looking more rested, she knew she was on the right track. What Liza didn't mention to anyone, including Jackie, was the therapy and medication she was taking. She supposed she better have a long talk with her cousin again. Jackie would be relieved that she went for help without her insisting this time. What Liza wasn't looking forward to was the conversation with Mr. Bonet. The trial date was right after Thanksgiving, and they would be meeting several times to go over everything. She hoped the therapist could help her between now and then. Time was running short.

25

Therapy was intense, but Liza knew it was exactly what she needed. With the trial coming up, they focused strictly on her abduction and the struggles that came afterward. Working through her anger and finding ways to cope with the tragedy were the most important things to cover. Dr. Peachtree increased her visits to three times a week, and they set the appointments before Liza went to work. That way she wouldn't be taking off so much time and causing difficulties with her work schedule. Although Liza knew that Mr. Jackson wouldn't mind due to the cause, she didn't want anyone at work to know what was going on.

Doing intense therapy before going to work was difficult. Liza was on an emotional rollercoaster, and it would take a good hour of work before she settled into the day. Cliff and Liza continued their weekly Wednesday meals, but she found herself pulling away from him again. Dr. Peachtree agreed Liza was so traumatized from the abduction that she couldn't give her relationship her full attention. The doctor encouraged her to be open and honest with Cliff about her struggles and to ask for time to work through the coming trial.

When the meeting time with Mr. Bonet's first visit arrived, Cliff offered to go with her. She almost agreed, just to have the emotional support in the room, but he was still livid with Nathan for locking her in that stupid closet, and Liza thought he might actually have a negative effect on her. Dr. Peachtree agreed. She could only deal with one thing at a time, and Cliff's emotions weren't it right now.

Mr. Bonet and Liza began by going over everything she remembered. Then they went over it repeatedly. Each time he expanded his questions to how she felt about being taken, tied up, and how scared she was while trying to walk down the cement stairs blindfolded. They talked about the smells, the darkness, and how she wasn't able to go to the bathroom without him watching. Of course, there was her physical state from starving and not having liquids, along with the chemicals affecting her nervous system. He asked her what she did with her time while locked up, and Liza explained how she tried to figure out who had abducted her and thought about all her loved ones, past and present. After three appointments, he said they would meet once more right before going into the courtroom and told her to enjoy her Thanksgiving. Liza barked out a laugh at the absurdity.

Jackie and Liza spent several hours preparing dishes for the holiday meal. They took that time to talk honestly about how Liza was doing. Dr. Peachtree kept telling her to share her trials, not hold them inside where it caused the turmoil. It was difficult, but she was beginning to understand the reasoning once she opened up to Jackie.

The weather turned ugly, and, although Jackie's parents arrived just before the storm hit, Cliff didn't make it out of town to his parents. He didn't mind coming over, of course. Ray and Cliff could always enjoy a football game or two, eating their way through the day. Aaron ran through the house like a mini-madman, and everyone enjoyed caring for him. Ray's parents lived in town, and they were also there to spend time with the festive group. When Liza began to think about the trial, Aaron was always a great distraction. Court was the following week, and Dr. Peachtree and Liza had one more session beforehand. She was going to need it.

*****

Cliff watched Liza become more closed off, lose weight, and make excuses about not getting together on the weekends. At least she continued to see him on Wednesday nights when she always appeared to have a good time. And then, just as suddenly, the dark rings were gone from under her eyes, and she looked like she was feeling better.

Always a little insecure in their relationship, Cliff worried they were headed backward again. He wanted nothing more than to marry Liza, but even Ray told him to back off. She had gone from a fun-loving person to quiet and withdrawn. He guessed he wasn't being fair, really. She had a lot of trauma recently. But Cliff wished Liza would let him give her more support. Jackie encouraged him to hold on and be patient until after the court hearing was over. Eventually, Liza had the same conversation with him.

"Cliff, I know I've been a little distant lately, but to be honest, I don't have the strength to deal with Nathan Lantry and build a relationship with you."

He sighed. "I just wish you would let me help you through this."

"Look, I didn't mention it before, because I wasn't sure how it would work out. Remember when I talked about seeing therapists in the past and had such terrible experiences?" Cliff nodded. "I went to see Dr. Moline a few weeks after my hospital stay. I wasn't sleeping and began to lose weight. Anyway, I'm back on an anti-depressant. He set me up with a great therapist, Dr. Peachtree, and I do Zoom calls two or three times a week. She has been fabulous and has helped me face a lot of my trauma."

"That's wonderful, honey. I'm glad you found someone to help you."

Liza gave Cliff a brief smile. "Right now, it's the abduction, but we've touched on all the rest. The one thing she reassured me of was that it was okay to handle one situation at a time and knew I wouldn't be able to do justice to our relationship. I need to get through this trial first."

Cliff reached over and took Liza's hands. Smiling, he pulled her a little closer. "Look. I'm here for you. It's difficult for me as I'm impatient and want to spend the rest of my life with you. But we have time to do this right, and I know that once Lantry lands behind bars for good, it will help us both feel better."

"I'm glad you understand. I do want us to continue building what we had started. It just seems like we get to a good place, and something happens to throw us back to square one. Evidently, I haven't faced my past completely, either. I've put it behind me, but I hid it all away instead of dealing with it. Dr. Peachtree is helping me, and I want to be able to give you the best me I can."

Cliff patted her hands. "I'll be here by your side, no matter how long it takes."

*****

Jackie had the babysitter come to the house so she could give her full attention to Liza during the trial. Liza took the week off work and planned to be in the courtroom for the whole thing. Dr. Peachtree knew she needed to face her abductor and face him she did. Every day.

Nathan's lawyer tried to play the sympathy card about his past drug use, being fired from his job, and that Nathan just wanted to retaliate against someone. Liza bravely gave her testimony while Mr. Bonet went over every small detail and emotion, just as they practiced. Three days later, the jury left the room and came back only a couple of hours later with a guilty verdict.

Relief flowed through Liza, and she and Cliff held tight to each other as she bawled her head off. Cliff almost cried more tears than she did. Jackie and Ray shed their own tears, and each hugged Liza for a moment. Eventually drying her tears, she was able to thank Mr. Bonet and the other lawyers for their time.

*****

Nathan would return for sentencing later, but his lawyer had done his best. He was guilty and now that he was sober again, he knew his sentence would be harsh. Not only kidnapping charges, but breaking and entering, assault, and drug charges.

Sarah continued to see Nathan in jail weekly. Between her visits and his AA meetings, he was finally coming to terms with how he ruined his life. He now knew he couldn't blame his wife, and definitely not Liza Augustine. He still felt a lot of anger about his family leaving town, but now that anger was directed at himself. Sarah helped him write a letter of apology to his wife for ruining their marriage. He didn't mail it right away because there was plenty of time. He just wasn't ready yet, either. Now that Nathan knew that he would be receiving a hefty sentence, there was no hope of going back to his former life. Without taking responsibility for his past mistakes, he knew there would be no future.

Back in court after the New Year, Nathan was sentenced to fifteen years with no early parole. Once back in his cell, he packed up his meager belongings and prepared to go to the state penitentiary. He looked at the letter to his wife once again, read it through, and prepared it for mailing. He had one more letter ready for Sarah and hoped she would visit occasionally. Last but not least, Nathan sat down and wrote a letter of apology to Liza. He hoped it would help find closure for them both. The cell door clanged open, he was cuffed and then led to the van leaving town. He took one last breath of fresh air, then calmly allowed himself to be shackled in place. Shaking his head, he felt like an idiot. Only a year ago, he had a fancy home, a wonderful family, and a fantastic job. He lost it all in a flash of pride and stupidity.

26

Liza wanted to be alone the evening after the trial. Once Jackie dropped her off at her apartment, she closed the door and leaned her back against it in relief. Taking a deep breath, she slowly made her way to the bathroom and peeled off her clothes in preparation for a hot shower. Standing under the running water, she let the cleansing tears wash away down the drain. Afterward, she wrapped herself in a big fluffy robe and then sat down and called Dr. Peachtree to discuss the outcome.

"It's over, except for the sentencing."

"How do you feel about it all now?"

"Relieved it's over and glad he was found guilty."

"How did you handle yourself? Did you crumble or not?"

"I did just fine. The coping techniques you taught me worked very well."

"Very good. Where do you want to go from here?"

"What do you mean?"

"We've touched on other stressors in your life, but if you remember right, we need to go over everything."

Liza let out a huge sigh. "I remember. Let's start from the beginning. Losing Jason and our child."

"Very good choice."

"Dr. Peachtree, I certainly appreciate everything, and I'm not sure I would have gotten this far without you."

"Pshaw. Honestly, Liza, you are stronger than you give yourself credit for. We've been working on coping mechanisms, and you seem to have found a clear path forward. Speaking of which, how is Cliff doing?"

Liza smiled. "He's been very supportive and has been trying to be patient with me. I may be ready to go forward now, thanks to you."

Dr. Peachtree smiled back. "Thanks for calling me and letting me know the outcome. We will visit about Jason during our next meeting."

"Bye. Thank you again."

Liza hung up and looked at the clock. Still early, she called Cliff. He answered on the first ring.

"Hey, sweetheart. Are you okay?"

"I'm great, actually. Have you eaten?"

"No. Not yet. Want me to come by and pick you up? We missed our usual date."

"That would be great. I'll meet you downstairs. I've showered and just need to get dressed."

"I'll be there shortly."

Liza rushed around and threw on a warm sweater and a good pair of jeans. Brushing her hair out, she blew it dry and tied it back out of the way. It had grown quite a bit in the last few months, and she hadn't done a thing about trimming it up. Cliff arrived shortly after Liza got to the front entrance. She threw on her coat and rushed to the car. Getting in, she leaned over and gave Cliff a long and passionate kiss. He was surprised but happy by her response. She was almost as surprised as he was. They both had stupid grins on their faces as they drove toward the café. Cliff kept driving and pulled into the parking lot of the same restaurant where they ate the night they first met.

"Wow. Going all out tonight, huh?"

"I decided we needed to celebrate your win."

Liza grinned. "You know what? You're right."

She jumped out of the car, and they went inside, arm

in arm. Cliff managed to get a table off to the side. They sat close to each other and chatted while waiting for their food.

"I haven't been here for ages."

"Me, either. Ray loves this place, but since Aaron was born, I'm not sure he's been back."

"We should babysit some night and let them get out. Their anniversary is coming up soon. How about then?"

"I'd love it. That Aaron has me wrapped around his little chubby fingers."

Liza laughed. "He has everyone at his beck and call. What a spoiled little guy he is."

The evening progressed and Liza loved every minute of it. Dr. Peachtree helped her through the trial, and she was ready to face life head-on now. And Cliff was going to be part of that life, no matter how much time they had left.

A few days later, Liza sat in front of her computer with her second cup of coffee. Outside of her call with Dr. Peachtree, she was ready for work. "Good morning, Doctor."

"Good morning. Let's get right to it. I know you don't like being late for work."

"I appreciate that."

"Tell me about the day Jason died. I want to know what you two did that morning and about the rest of your day. Now think back to when you were still home together. I know that was a long time ago, but bear with me."

"That was several years ago. Let me see."

Liza sat back and almost closed her eyes, looked toward the ceiling, and thought about that morning. It took a few minutes to get the proper order of things together as she mulled everything over in her mind before speaking.

Liza waved her hands around as she described the day. "I fixed us both breakfast, and we talked about what our day was going to be like. I still wasn't working, and I had an appointment with the lawyer later that day about the sexual harassment case. Jason was going to work as usual." She looked at Dr. Peachtree. "I don't remember anything unusual happening."

"Okay. Was Jason going to come with you to your appointment?"

She waved her hands around again in dismissal. "Oh, no. He said he would take off early to go with me, but I told him it wasn't a big deal. He and I had been over the issue several times, and the visit with the lawyer was going to solidify all the information into building my case. I figured there would be plenty of time for him to sit with me, especially if we went to court."

"All right. So, what happened after breakfast?"

"I cleaned up the apartment, fixed myself some lunch, then took a shower before dressing for the appointment."

"And Jason?"

"He went to work."

"And did he ask about coming to the appointment again before leaving?"

"Hmmm. I think he did, but I just poo-pooed him off and told him I could call if I needed him."

"So now you are ready for your appointment."

"Yes. I drove over to the lawyer's office and sat for a few moments, then was called back. We were going over everything when my phone rang. That's when I noticed it was the police, so I took the call. I'm glad I did. I left the office and went right to the hospital."

"And you got there before he died and were able to talk to him a bit."

"Yes. I will always be grateful we were able to say we loved each other."

"Now. I have a few things I want to go over. You stated you felt that great loss, and then two weeks later you miscarried, which was probably due to the stress of Jason's accident."

Liza nodded. "I didn't know I was pregnant. We didn't know. Although we had been trying since I was fired from my job. We thought that was a perfect time to have a family since I wasn't working anyway."

"I know you two were very much in love. I pulled the accident report. Have you ever wondered why Jason was on the highway at that time of day?"

Liza paused. "I hadn't given it any thought, but it was too early for him to come home."

"I tried to decide if I should tell you this or not, but I considered that you may have repressed these memories. Jason told the police that he was on his way to an appointment to meet his wife. If he had stayed at work like you asked, he wouldn't have been in that wreck."

"Oh no!" Liza looked devastated, her eyes wide, her mouth dropped open, and she acted as if she couldn't catch her breath. After some time, she leaned back and brushed a few tears away. "Yes. I did know that. And yes, I pushed the thoughts away. I didn't want to blame Jason for dying. I didn't want to blame him for not staying at work and getting in the middle of the wreck that killed him. I believe his parents understood what really happened and why. But they wanted to blame me since I was the one who was filing the suit. Blame doesn't bring anyone back. We ended up sticking together in the end, but we aren't close now. I was so devastated at the time; I don't think I even noticed they were in as bad a shape as me." She shook her head. "Of course they were. Jason was their son. I haven't talked to them in a long time. In fact, I think the last time I saw them was when I cleaned out Jason's things and asked them to come pick up some mementos I thought they would like to have. Jason kept a box of stuff from high school and college, and I had no use for them."

Dr. Peachtree watched silently as Liza worked through the events of that awful day and was pleased to see her dealing with the information as well as she had. "Things are not always as they seem after tragic events. A person only remembers what they want. Sometimes, all people talk about is how they were wronged and how it affected them personally. I know people who have been blaming others for years. It doesn't solve anything, nor does it help a person get on with their life. In your case, you withdrew and didn't cope with life at all. You operated like a robot until Jackie helped you walk away from the past and toward the here and now." She smiled. "I'd like to meet that cousin of yours sometime."

Liza returned the smile. "She is wonderful."

"How do you feel about the loss of Jason and your child now? Are you still harboring a fear of further commitment to Cliff?"

"I think that the forced stay in the closet changed my perspective on that, for sure. I still have moments when I worry, but those thoughts are fleeting now. All the work we've done the last few weeks has certainly helped me. Cliff has a failed relationship in his past that made him such a skeptic about relationships that he hadn't even dated for several years. I think we are finding our way forward, together."

"That's good to hear. Do you want to discuss your parent's and brother's death this visit or wait until next time?"

"Honestly? I don't think I need to talk about it at all. My family is gone, and nothing can bring them back. I was dealt a lot to handle in a few short years, including being on death's door. I was worrying too much about dealing with another possible death, I didn't even think about my own demise until it hit me in the face." She let out a large sigh. "When I went toward the light, Jason told me it wasn't my time. So, when it is, he will be waiting for me along with my other family members. I know this now."

"Very good. Let's wrap this up for the day, and we will visit later in the week. It sounds like we will be able to cut you back to once a week until you and I can agree we are done. I don't want to cut you loose too soon. Sometimes things come up in your everyday life that sparks a repressed memory or two, and we can deal with it when we need to."

"Great. Someday, I'm going to meet you in person. Dr. Moline was right. You are a peach." The doctor laughed, and they disconnected the call.

Liza made her way to work and smiled as she thought about Dr. Peachtree's session. She had come a long way, and the darkness was no longer crowding the edges of her life. Cliff was a bright spot, and even though they had a rough start to their relationship, they had built a stronger one because of it.

*****

The holidays were over, Nathan had been sentenced, and Liza was back to work and feeling stronger than ever. Pierre called one day and asked if he and his family could come to see her in a few months. Now that the company's division was saved and things were humming along, he wanted to bring Felicia and their little one to the States. She encouraged him to wait until spring and was sure that Jackie would be happy to have a neighborhood BBQ again. Smiling, she hung up and thought about Jackie and Ray. They were expecting their second child, and what better way to celebrate than by having another BBQ?

Jackie's parents arrived to babysit so the two couples could go out for Valentine's Day. They went to their favorite restaurant and were having a fabulous time. The place was filled with happy couples enjoying a night on the town. Cliff ordered desserts for the table, even though both couples were stuffed. When the waitress arrived, Liza's dessert was in the shape of a heart with a gift attached. Looking around, Liza didn't see the rest of the tables having desserts like hers and wondered about it aloud. Ray told her it must be one gift per table type of thing and to open it so everyone could see. She shrugged and peeled off the paper. Opening the box, there was another small box inside. She pulled out the velvet box and snapped it open. Inside was a beautiful engagement ring. In awe, she finally realized Cliff was kneeling beside her. He gently took the ring out of the box, then placed it on Liza's finger.

"This might be a little presumptuous of me, but would you be my wife? And soon?"

She smiled at Cliff and then threw her arms around him. "Yes. Oh, yes!" The diners whooped and hollered.

After a big, mushy kiss, Cliff stood up and pulled Liza

with him. "Thank heavens. It's about time." The people sitting closest to them laughed, along with Ray and Jackie.

He whispered. "Let's elope."

Liza pulled back and looked into his eyes. "Yes. Let's." Cliff let out another loud whoop and everyone laughed again.

*****

May turned into a beautiful month. The weather had cooperated for the BBQ, and Cliff was actually civil to Pierre. After all, Liza married him, not Pierre. Jackie was beginning to show, and Aaron was running around the yard and under everyone's feet. He was quite the little socializer. Cliff and Liza stuck to each other like glue most of the time.

Ray came over and pulled Cliff away from his bride. "Come man the grill with me and let that woman breathe."

Liza laughed and shoved Cliff toward Ray. Not as many people were invited to this shindig, but there were still plenty of people around. She walked over to where Jackie and her mother were visiting with the neighbors. Felicia was with them.

"So, what do you think of our BBQ? Anything like what Pierre described?"

"I love it. I think he exaggerated a bit the more he told the story, though."

"I believe it. But this party isn't quite as grand as the first one. So maybe he didn't exaggerate too much."

They chatted for a long time, then Pierre came to sweep Felicia off her feet to dance. Eventually, Cliff came back and gave her a hug and whispered in Liza's ear.

"Are you about ready to tell them?"

"Sure."

Cliff grinned, tugged Liza with him, walked to where the band was playing, and borrowed a microphone. "Hey, everyone. Thanks for coming and helping Ray and Jackie celebrate the coming of their next family member." Everyone clapped and whistled. When it quieted down, Cliff continued. "For those that may not know, Liza and I got married on March first." Another round of celebratory clapping was heard. Cliff and Liza were both grinning from ear to ear. Cliff continued as soon as he could talk over the crowd noise. "What all of you don't know is, we are going to have a baby this fall."

Everyone roared with congratulations once again. Ray, Jackie, Pierre, and Felicia came running over and took turns hugging and congratulating the couple. Dr. Peachtree and her husband attended, along with Dr. Moline and his wife. Liza was so happy to meet Dr. Peachtree in person. They had discontinued her therapy sessions at the end of February, but the doctor was available for Liza at any time if needed.

The music eventually got started once again, and the couple wandered off. The little ones were dancing to the music, and the whole neighborhood enjoyed the festivities for another hour. Pierre eventually took his family to the motel, and the neighbors began to go home. Cliff and Ray cleaned up the grill, while Jackie, her mom, and Liza put away the leftovers. The BBQ was a success once again.

As Cliff and Liza walked to their car to leave, she looked up at the stars and took a deep breath. Thinking back to the previous year, her life had certainly changed. Happiness is what you make it, and she certainly was happy. Getting in the car, she smiled at Cliff, patted her tummy, and was deeply grateful for her life and family.

About the Author

Diane Winters is from Southwest Nebraska and is an avid reader of all genres. She came from a large family and grew up in a farming community. She was blessed with two children and has four grandchildren of her own. Diane has been a nurse for many years and held various positions in the healthcare field over time.

Diane appreciates the sunsets, rainstorms, rainbows, and views from the mountaintops. She and her husband enjoy traveling, and the drive time gives Diane the opportunity to work out new storylines.

www.facebook.com/DianeLWinters
https://www.amazon.com/stores/Diane-Winters/author/B01M9HRNPF?ref=ap_rdr&store_ref=ap_rdr&isDramIntegrated=true&shoppingPortalEnabled=true

Other books from Blossom Spring Publishing:

City Girls to Prairie Girls
No One Lives Forever
Finding Meg
Mending Fences

www.blossomspringpublishing.com